BRENDAN BUCKLEY'S
SIXTH-GRADE EXPERIMENT

P9-DDI-192

Sundee T. Frazier

A Yearling Book

Text copyright © 2012 by Sundee T. Frazier
Cover art copyright © 2012 by Robert Papp

All rights reserved. Published in the United States by Yearling, an imprint of Random House Children's Books, a division of Random House, Inc., New York. Originally published in hardcover in the United States by Delacorte Press, an imprint of Random House Children's Books, New York, in 2012.

Yearling and the jumping horse design are registered trademarks of Random House, Inc.

Visit us on the Web! randomhouse.com/kids
Educators and librarians, for a variety of teaching tools, visit us at RHTeachersLibrarians.com

The Library of Congress has cataloged the hardcover edition of this work as follows:
Frazier, Sundee Tucker.
Brendan Buckley's sixth-grade experiment / Sundee T. Frazier.—1st ed.
p. cm.
Sequel to: Brendan Buckley's universe and everything in it.
Summary: As biracial Brendan Buckley enters middle school, he deals with issues with his African American father, a new girl at school, and his changing friendship with his best friend.
ISBN 978-0-385-74050-0 (hc)
ISBN 978-0-375-89930-0 (ebook)
ISBN 978-0-375-98949-0 (glb)
[1. Racially mixed people—Fiction. 2. Interpersonal relations—Fiction. 3. Fathers and sons—Fiction. 4. Science projects—Fiction. 5. Middle schools—Fiction. 6. Schools—Fiction.] I. Title.
PZ7.F8715Br 2012
[Fic]—dc22
2011009377

ISBN 978-0-385-74051-7 (pbk.)

Printed in the United States of America

To Matt—
for fifteen years of commitment,
passion, partnership, and most
definitely, fun

CHAPTER 1

My green anole has no table manners. He munches crickets like my best friend, Khalfani, eats Pringles. Mouth wide open. Crunching them so hard and fast, they're gone in no time flat. With Khal, it's gross. But with my lizard, Einstein, it's *amazing*. In fact, it may be the coolest thing I've ever seen.

I'd watched Einstein chase and devour his food six times since I'd gotten him a couple of weeks before—a gift from my parents for my eleventh birthday—and it had been exciting every time. I'd recorded every single cricket he'd eaten in my brand-new green spiral notebook.

Across the cover of the notebook, I'd written my anole's name, EINSTEIN, and on the title page,

The Life and Times of a Green Anole
by Brendan S. Buckley

I planned to record everything about keeping my new pet. I'd made sections for six categories and marked them with little sticky tabs I'd found in Mom's desk: *Feeding, Tank Temps* (which I would be checking every day until I was sure I wasn't accidentally going to roast or freeze him to death), *Behavior, Other Observations, Research*, and the most important one of all—*Questions*.

Some people never ask questions. Maybe they're afraid they'll look dumb, or maybe they don't think of things to ask. But not me. It's like my brain is one big bowl of Rice Krispies and all my questions are the milk. It's a constant *snap*, *crackle*, and *pop* up there.

Mom encourages all my inquiries and investigations. But Dad has his limits. "Enough with the questions, Brendan," he'll say. But I can never stop asking questions. It's just what scientists do.

I sat on my bed and opened my notebook to the section titled *Research*. Here's what I'd written down so far:

- Anoles eat grubs, crickets, cockroaches, spiders, moths—any arthropod that will fit in their mouths. (Arthropod: any of a phylum—Arthropoda—of invertebrate animals, such as insects, arachnids, and crustaceans, that have a segmented body and jointed appendages.)
- Don't feed them anything bigger than one-half the size of their heads!

- Insects caught in the wild may be accepted eagerly. (Cool! Try this out!)

I created another bullet point for the information I hadn't had time to record the night before. Dad may be the stricter parent, but when it comes to eating healthy food and sticking to bedtimes, Mom turns into the Enforcer. I wrote down what I had read on The ReptileZone.com, a site for herpetologists like me:

- Green anoles turn brown when stressed. Causes of stress: temperature in tank too hot or cold; too much handling.

Next, I flipped to the *Feeding* section and made my seventh entry: "Saturday, September 1, 8:00 a.m." I'd learned from the man at the pet store that if you fed your anole at the same time every day, he'd start showing up early for the grub.

I pulled out my cricket keeper from under the table we'd set up to hold the twenty-gallon tank. The tank was against the wall closest to the foot of my bed, next to the door. I stared into the plastic case at the few remaining crickets. They weren't called pinheads for nothing. They were practically microscopic. "Sorry, guys, I'm back."

I felt a little bad for the insects. Their only reason for

existing was to serve as lizard chow. But then again, that's what the food chain is all about. The big guys eat the little guys. Then the even bigger guys come along and eat *them*. That's life. Something has to die so something else can live.

I slid out one of the black tubes from the keeper and shook several crickets into a plastic Baggie. I scooped up one spoonful of vitamin powder and dumped it in with the crickets. Then I shook the bag to coat them.

"Mmm-*hmm*. Just like your Grampa Clem's favorite, Shake 'n Bake!" my Grandma Gladys had said the first time she'd seen me feed Einstein. It had made me wish that Grampa Clem could have been there. He would have thought that watching a lizard eat crickets was one of the coolest things he'd ever seen, too.

I had just lifted the wire-mesh top to dump in Einstein's meal when I heard Grandpa Ed's truck door slam in our driveway. He was there to pick me up for my first official rock expedition with the Puyallup Rock Club. A whole day in the mountains to dig for quartz crystals. We were even camping overnight!

I quickly closed the tank's lid, set the supplement container on the mouth of the cricket Baggie so the little buggers wouldn't get away, and headed for the door. "I got it!" I shouted. I took the stairs two at a time.

"Did I miss breakfast?" Grandpa Ed held up a baby-food jar filled with wood shavings. "I brought Einstein a treat."

I took the jar and peered inside. "Mealworms! Thanks!" I closed the door.

"And another batch of crickets for you." He held up a container full of pinheads hopping all over each other. "Well, I mean, for your lizard."

"Yeah. I've heard they taste pretty good fried, but I think I'll let Einstein have them." I smiled.

Grandpa Ed chuckled.

"And you didn't miss anything. I was just about to feed him."

We met Dad at the top of the stairs, headed into the kitchen. He was in his police uniform already. The edges of his hairline and goatee looked as if they'd been created with an X-Acto knife. He smelled like his aftershave—like spicy pine trees. "Hello there, Ed. How you doing this morning?"

"Couldn't be better. Been looking forward to this time with my grandson for the last three weeks." We smiled at each other.

Dad stepped over to the coffeemaker. "Coffee for the road?"

"Thanks, I've got some in the truck. Sorry you're not able to join us. Would've been great to have you along."

I tugged on Grandpa Ed's sleeve. "Come on, Grandpa. I'm trying to train Einstein to come out every morning at eight." I didn't feel like hearing Dad's excuses for why he wasn't coming as he'd said he would.

Dad's spoon clanked against the side of his travel

mug. "Yeah, I thought it might work out, but then I got my first reading assignment. I'm not the quick study Brendan is." He looked at me with a raised eyebrow and a half smile. I looked at my socked feet. "So while you're hitting the mountainside, I'll be hitting the books."

Dad had enrolled in a program to finish his bachelor's degree. It was something he said Grampa Clem had been disappointed with him about—dropping out of college. Plus, he couldn't advance any further in the police department without it.

I tugged Grandpa Ed's sleeve again.

"Maybe another time, then," Grandpa Ed said. He pulled his arm from my grasp and put his hand on my shoulder. He was trying to get me to be patient, but I didn't have time for this.

"Yeah, maybe."

Probably not was more like it.

"I'm glad for you two to get some time together, though." Dad screwed the lid on the coffee mug. He picked up his keys and wallet from the counter. "Have a good time, Brendan. See you tomorrow." He ruffled my hair, which has looser curls and is never as neat as his.

"Okay. Bye." As soon as Dad was past us on the stairs, I pulled Grandpa Ed to my room at the end of the hall. Einstein was sitting near the front of the tank. "He's waiting for his food," I whispered. I didn't want to scare him back into the fake ivy.

I lifted the lid and shook the calcium-coated crickets

in. The first one's legs had barely touched the bark on the bottom of the tank before Einstein snatched it up. "Whoa!" Grandpa Ed said. "I'd say the feller was hungry."

The other crickets hopped away. Catching them would give Einstein a chance to get some exercise, after he finished the one clamped in his jaws. He munched and chewed, mouth opening wide between bites.

"He needs some work on his table manners," I said, thinking of Dad, who is a stickler about chewing with your mouth closed and not talking while you eat, something I sometimes find hard to do.

Grandpa Ed chuckled. "Maybe so, but I don't see it happening. Now, if you put a *lady* lizard in there . . ."

"Nah. Einstein's going to be a bachelor. He'll be happier that way."

"You don't think he'll get lonely while you're off at school all day?"

"I researched it. Green anoles are more or less solitary in the wild. Plus, I was lucky even to get *one* anole. Mom had to work pretty hard to convince Dad." Einstein had been cheap, but all his gear—not so much. There was the tank, of course, and then three different kinds of lamps, thermometers (for both the cool and warm sides of the tank), a hygrometer, fake plants, a couple of real plants, substrate to line the bottom (which has to be changed regularly)—even a trip to the reptile vet. The guy at the pet store recommended it since Einstein had been captured in the wild, just to make sure he was free of parasites and all that.

Dad had complained when we'd gotten the vet's bill in the mail. "You've got to be kidding me!" Then he practically made me swear on Grampa Clem's grave that I wouldn't kill Einstein through neglect. "Ignorance is also no excuse. You're smart. After all this money, you'd better figure *out* how to keep this animal alive."

The only thing we hadn't bought was the big rock I'd found at the park and put in Einstein's tank for a basking spot, which was where he was lying now, after having polished off a second cricket.

I opened the container of mealworms and plucked one out. It wriggled in my fingers. I dropped it near the rock. "Here you go, Einstein. Dessert on Grandpa Ed. See you tomorrow."

He lifted his long, thin snout in the air as if sniffing the new presence in his tank. His white-spotted pink throat fan shot out from his bright lime-colored body, warning other anoles to stay away. This was his territory, his grub. Of course, he didn't have to worry. There was no one there but him. He would learn soon enough. I just hoped he would be happy in his new home. And that I wouldn't accidentally kill him.

I recorded the crickets and the mealworm in my notebook, misted the tank with purified water from the spray bottle Mom had given me, then put away the feeding stuff and grabbed my backpack. On my way out the door, I reached up to the shelf above Einstein's tank, where I kept the rock and mineral collection I'd started this summer. I touched the glass-lidded wood box Grandpa Ed had made me for my birthday. Inside sat the chunk of Ellensburg Blue agate that we'd found on our last expedition—a secret outing that had almost gotten Grandpa Ed killed.

Bring me luck, I thought. I wanted to come home with something big. Something impressive. Something that might even make Dad regret skipping the trip.

CHAPTER 2

After I'd reminded Mom about all the things she needed to do for Einstein while I was gone ("Turn on the nocturnal heat lamp at night, check and record tank temps, mist the leaves, and put in a piece of apple to keep any leftovers alive—anoles only eat live prey"), finally, *finally*, we were going!

I'd been counting down since my birthday, and now, after twelve days, eight hours, and twenty-eight minutes, there we were, sitting in the cab of Grandpa Ed's truck with our camping gear and rock-hounding tools in back, waving goodbye to Mom.

Patches Junior ran circles in the bed of the truck. He jumped up with his paws on the cab's rear window, barked, and then lay down for the ride, safe under the camper shell.

"Have fun, Bren!" Mom called. She was still in her

robe and her hair was smooshed up on one side from sleeping on it, but that's a good thing about my mom—she doesn't spend hours making her hair and face look perfect, like some moms. She'd rather be outside playing ball, or watch me do Tae Kwon Do, or hear about my latest experiment. "And be careful!" she shouted as we drove off.

Mom didn't need to tell me to have fun—or to be careful, for that matter. On our last expedition, the secret one, not only had Grandpa Ed almost died, I'd smashed up his truck trying to find help. The hood's been fixed, but let's just say I won't be driving anything—not even one of those motorized chairs at Gladys's senior living community—until I'm legal.

This time, though, there were no secrets. Mom was happy I was going, which was a big turnaround from the previous month, when she had forbidden me even to *see* my grandpa, her dad. I had discovered him at a rock show the month before that, after not knowing him my whole life (he and Mom hadn't been speaking). But everyone had made up since then. Everything was good. The only thing that could have been better was if Dad had been with us, heading toward the mountains.

I'd called my bud Khal to see if he wanted to go instead.

"And risk getting eaten by a cougar or sweating to death—for a few rocks? No thanks, man." He said he'd be thinking of me from the safety and comfort of his air-conditioned bedroom while he dug virtual tunnels in Mario World.

Summers *had* been getting hotter in the Pacific Northwest over the past few years. I'd done some research on the whole global warming thing, and I was convinced from the data it was real.

As we zoomed along Highway 18 toward the Cascades and Snoqualmie Pass, I refocused on being with my grandpa, doing something we both liked to do—hunt for rocks. Sitting there next to Grandpa Ed, I thought about Grampa Clem again, which I still did kind of a lot. I supposed the hurt of him dying wasn't as deep as it had been a few months before. It helped that I'd found Grandpa Ed. Although he could never replace Grampa Clem, he was fun to be with, and he gave me that same safe feeling Grampa Clem had. That feeling that you're not just a twig getting blown around by the wind, but a branch that belongs to a big tree that stands tall and proud and has been standing tall and proud for a long, long time.

Grandpa Ed handed me a map. Not a normal street map with freeways and town names. This one showed rivers and trails and elevations marked with different colors. "A geological survey map," he said. "We'll be right here." He tapped a section of the grid with his finger. I scanned the map, trying to figure it out, but it was all new to me.

It didn't really matter. We would get there eventually, and when we did, I was going to dig up some huge quartz crystals!

But first, I had to dig for some food. My stomach felt like a giant sinkhole—something I'd read about on the Internet recently. Sinkholes forms when underground water dissolves subterranean rock until the surface land has no support and collapses. During the Civil War, a sinkhole in Kentucky swallowed up three Confederate soldiers! I wasn't *that* hungry, but I could eat.

I plowed through the bag of snacks Mom had packed. "Want one?" I asked, holding up an energy bar.

Grandpa Ed glanced at the wrapper. "Those marketing yahoos sure know how to sucker people."

I studied the packaging. "What do you mean?"

"Those things don't give you any more energy than a good old-fashioned donut, and they don't taste even a quarter as good. Tried one once. Tasted about as good as a dried cow patty."

"Have you actually tasted a dried cow patty?"

"Don't need to. Remember, son . . ." Grandpa Ed's pointer finger tapped against my temple. "Imagination. It's more important than knowledge." He'd first told me that Albert Einstein quote one of the times I'd snuck over to his house, before he and Mom made up.

Grandpa Ed opened the white paper bag between us and pulled out a gooey donut. "I'll stick with my *maple* bars, thanks."

I dropped the energy bar into the sack and picked

out a donut. What Mom didn't know wouldn't hurt me.
"Speaking of dried cow patties and energy," I said, biting
into the sugary frosting, "I've been reading about biofuels
and biogas."

"Oh yeah? Why's that?"

"Just curious. You know, the whole global warming
thing."

I couldn't tell from his "Hmmm" whether he would
agree with me that it was a real problem, or if he thought
it was a whole lot of hoo-ha over nothing, as he would say.

"Did you know that in twenty-four hours a cow burps
and farts enough methane to run your house's furnace
for the same amount of time?"

Grandpa Ed's eyes got big. "That's some serious
power. I suppose you could call it Holstein heat."

I groaned.

"How 'bout Jersey juice?"

Another bad one. I shook my head.

"Bovine burn?"

I laughed. "They're getting worse." I thought for a
moment. "I know! Cow kilowatts!"

We both laughed at that.

"I have a lot of questions about the subject, of
course."

"Of course."

I'd recorded my questions in my science notebook—
Brendan Buckley's Book of Big Questions About Life, the

Universe and Everything In It—which I'd started keeping at the beginning of the summer and had tucked into my backpack for this trip.

"Questions are good. They're what keep us scientists searching, eh?" Grandpa Ed smiled at me with his blue eyes—sky-blue, like the water in one of those sinkholes.

I nodded. This summer I'd gained not only a grandpa but also someone in my own family who shared my interest in science. I sat back and licked the frosting from my fingers. This was going to be great.

Someone had beaten us to the campsite. A green Subaru Forester sat in the parking area. Over by some picnic tables, a man worked at pitching a rounded blue tent.

Our tires crunched on the gravel. Grandpa Ed pulled up and parked.

A girl's head popped up from behind the tent. She looked straight at me and smiled. It was that girl . . . the one from the rock club meeting I'd attended with Grandpa Ed earlier in the summer.

What was her name? My mind was blank.

P.J. clawed at the windows and whined. I grabbed my backpack and headed to the rear of the truck. The pine trees smelled good—much better than they did as pulp. Factories in Tacoma cook trees like these down to mush and pump out a smell like rotten eggs. People like to joke about the "aroma of Tacoma." I took another deep breath of clean, piney air.

The girl walked toward me. Galloped was more like it. "Hi, Brendan!"

Uh-oh. She remembered my name. I hoped my deodorant was ready for a challenge, because I could feel the sweat beads forming on my upper lip and under my arms. Dad had given me the deodorant this summer to help with the girls, he said. I hadn't had a chance to tell him that girls were about as far from my mind as Pluto is from the sun. He'd left too quickly.

Suddenly, the brown-haired girl was at my side, all excited and bouncy, like Silly Putty.

"Oh . . . uh . . . hi." I kept my eyes on P.J. as I lowered the tailgate. He jumped out of the truck and trotted off to sniff the ground around Grandpa Ed, who was talking with the girl's dad. I remembered seeing him at the meeting, too.

"I was hoping you'd be here," she said.

She was? "You were?"

"Yes. I have something for you."

"You do?" I hadn't thought about this girl one time since the meeting, but she'd obviously been thinking about me.

The girl ran to the Subaru and leaned through the back window.

I wracked my brain for her name, like I was digging

through my closet for one of Dad's tools after borrowing it for an experiment. I had a feeling that forgetting a girl's name was the kind of thing that could get a boy in serious trouble. I might not have been thinking about girls all that much, but that didn't mean I hadn't observed some things about them. Observing is what scientists do.

She returned with a chunk of kidney ore. She'd had a specimen just like it at the meeting. We'd talked about it . . . how hematite's streak is dark red, like blood, even though it's black on the outside. *Never judge a rock by its color*, she'd said.

"Hematite," I said.

She handed me the mineral. I felt its rough edges. Its bumpy surface gleamed. "Is this the one from your collection?"

"No. I got this one just for you. I had a feeling I'd be seeing you again—since you're the rock club president's grandson and all." She smiled with her lips closed.

My face got hot, and not from the sun beating down on us from above the treetops. I hadn't been sure she'd believed me about being Grandpa Ed's grandson, since he hadn't introduced me that way at the meeting. "Oh. Uh . . . thanks."

"Isn't the botryoidal habit amazing?"

Habit? What kind of habit would a mineral have? I examined the hematite as if I knew exactly what she meant. "Uh, sure." I shuffled my feet, trying to think of some way to escape her stare, which was as intense as the sun's rays.

"Morgan!" her dad called.

Morgan. I was saved—in more ways than one. She turned toward her dad.

"Ready to finish the job?" He held up the rubber mallet he'd been using to pound the tent stakes.

Grandpa Ed said something and slapped the man's back. They laughed. Another car arrived with two men inside.

Morgan turned to me, grinning. "We're going to have so much fun!" She bounded back to the tent. I stood there holding the hematite, not sure what had just happened.

Grandpa Ed came and started pulling supplies from the back of the truck. "Got yourself a girlfriend?"

I shoved the mineral into my pocket. Hopefully he wouldn't ask what it was. "I don't even know her!"

He smiled slightly and slicked his orangish-gray hair away from his forehead. "Don't go getting your boxers in a wad." He handed me the large canvas bag of digging tools. "Take this, will you?"

I slung the bag over my shoulder and practically fell over backward. I glanced in Morgan's direction, then quickly looked back to Ed, hoping he hadn't noticed me checking to see if she'd seen me stumble. Fortunately, he was fiddling with a knob on his Coleman stove.

"Morgan's been coming to our meetings all summer. Smart girl. Her dad says she's been hounding since she was knee-high. What more could a boy ask for?"

Grandpa Ed pulled out our tent and walked to a spot about ten yards from Morgan and her dad. I dragged the bag of tools behind me, scowling. I wasn't asking for *anything*—not a piece of hematite and definitely not a girlfriend.

I'd have to make sure no one got the wrong idea about Morgan and me. *Girlfriend?* Not in a million years!

CHAPTER 3

A few hours later, the ten of us on the expedition were spread out along a steep hillside. Scraggly pine trees shaded us, but it was still super-hot. We crouched over screens, panning for crystals like prospectors during the gold rush. I had to use all my Tae Kwon Do balancing skills to keep from sliding down the rocky slope.

My grandpa, the expedition leader, had shown me where to dig and how to move the sand and pebbles through the quarter-inch screen. Quartz fragments littered the ground, but so far I'd only found a couple worth keeping—one about three-quarters the size of my pinky; the other, half the size of that.

I set the screen on the ground, took off my baseball cap, and swiped my forehead with my arm. Panning for crystals was about as slow going as fishing, but with way more work involved! I had never broken a sweat sitting on the pier with Grampa Clem.

Grandpa Ed handed me the flask. I took a swig of water. He pointed to some rock outcroppings. "Granite," he said. "You're looking at the Snoqualmie Batholith right there—a huge igneous rock formation, mostly underground. We can see it thanks to erosion and uplift."

Morgan piped up from where she balanced nearby, still shaking her screen. "My dad and I read about that. The batholith was formed in the late Oligocene epoch, twenty-eight *million* years ago! It's teeming with minerals."

I'd read the same thing, preparing for our trip.

"Absolutely right!" Grandpa Ed winked at her. "That girl of yours is sharp as a tack, John. Sharp as a tack."

I pulled my cap down low on my head and went back to digging. So she'd read a few things. What was so sharp about that?

"Don't I know it." Morgan's dad leaned on the end of his shovel. "Keeps her mom and me on our toes, that's for sure."

I grabbed my screen and started sifting. I was determined to find something big. Something Grandpa Ed would say was a real find. Something I could take home and show Dad.

A glint in the dirt caught my eye. I swiped at the topsoil, uncovering a rounded whitish rock almost as big as a baseball. Sparkly flecks on the rock gleamed, even in the shadows. Was it some kind of mica? Could it be muscovite?

"Grandpa! I think I found something!" I held up the rock. He stepped over and took the specimen.

"Hmmm . . . yes."

"Is it muscovite?" Excitement built in my chest.

Grandpa Ed turned the rock over in his hand. "This right here is what we'd call . . . a throw-it-at-your-cat rock." He and a few of the guys standing nearby laughed. He plopped the dumb thing back into my palm. I glanced around, feeling as hot as if the granite around us were still magma and not hardened rock. Morgan kneeled with her back to us, intently shaking her screen. She didn't appear to have heard the joke.

"Sorry, kiddo." Grandpa Ed thumped my back. "Keep looking."

A few minutes later, Morgan cried out, "Look at this!" She held up a large chunk of something. It didn't look like much. Probably just a big dirt clod around a few tiny crystals.

Grandpa Ed hiked over to where she stood. I stayed put. I could see fine from where I was, and I was sure what I'd see would be the clump breaking up in Grandpa Ed's hands. *Too bad*, I'd say. *Better luck next time*.

"Mind if I take a look?" Grandpa Ed took the dried-mud-covered whatever it was and knocked off as much dirt as he could. He spit on it a few times and rubbed it against his shirt. He held it up again. "Well, how about that? You found yourself a *real* beaut!"

A couple of men and one of the women digging and sifting nearby stopped their work to see what Grandpa Ed was making such a big deal about.

I inched over, still not believing the clump of crystals could be as big as it looked. Grandpa Ed pointed to the large center crystal. Its end was purple-tinged. "Looky here."

"Is that *amethyst?*" Morgan asked. She sounded in awe of her own find.

No way, I thought.

"You bet," Grandpa Ed said.

Morgan's and my eyes opened wide at the same time.

Grandpa Ed patted Morgan's shoulder as he handed back the crystals. She held up the specimen for her dad to see. He smiled and nodded in approval.

"I haven't seen a cluster that impressive in at least two or three years," Grandpa Ed said.

Two or three *years?* The odds of me discovering anything close to what this girl had found were suddenly a big fat zero. She had gotten my specimen. The huge one *I* was going to find!

Morgan smiled from ear to ear. Her mouth seemed almost too big for her face. "Do you want to see it, Brendan?" She held out the quartz. The amethyst-tinged quartz.

Of course I did. But I couldn't bring myself to say so.

Morgan came closer with the cluster, still holding it out. I took it in my hands, solid, heavy. Purple, like my Tae Kwon Do belt, which stood for "growing nobly toward harvest." I imagined myself running and sliding down the hillside with the crystals in my hand.

And then what? Making a getaway in Grandpa Ed's truck? Not exactly what I'd call noble.

I gave her back her find. My mouth said, "Sweet," but my mood had turned sour.

After another half hour or so, we headed to a different site in the same area. I dug for a little while, but when I wasn't finding much, I threw sticks for P.J. to fetch, until he got bored and wandered off. So then I got out my notebook and tried to think up some more Big Questions, like "What makes amethyst purple?" and "How does deodorant work?" and "Could cow farts actually heat homes?"

Finally, we all hiked back to the campsite. While the others crowded around Morgan's specimen, the biggest catch of the day, I stayed near our tent, using a metal brush to scrub the few measly pieces I had to show for all my work. At least P.J. didn't care about Morgan's "amazing" amethyst. He lay at my feet, pooped from all his exploring and retrieving. I nicked my knuckles on the brass bristles and winced.

Grandpa Ed kneeled next to me. "I'd say those are about as clean as you're going to get them."

"Yeah, I guess."

He put his hand on the back of my neck. "Remember, finding minerals is one part skill, one part knowledge, and two parts luck. We'll have better luck next time."

"Sure." I kept my eyes on my crystal fragments.

"This one right here's a solid find." He picked up the nearly clear crystal that was almost the size of my pinky. "Nice hexagonal form . . . not too cloudy."

I tried to see the specimen for what it was instead of in comparison to anyone else's. Grandpa Ed was right. It wasn't so bad. It was pretty cool, actually. And I'd dug it myself.

Dinner was potluck style. Grandpa Ed fired up his Coleman stove, then went to his truck and brought back the most gigantic can of baked beans I'd ever seen in my life. Mom had sent me with fruit salad to share. Everyone put their food on the picnic table.

I filled my plate and sat in one of the low-to-the-ground folding chairs near the fire ring we'd made. I was working hard to keep my paper plate from sagging in the middle so that I wouldn't end up with a fruity baked-bean mess. I didn't like my foods to touch.

Morgan sat in the chair next to mine—the one I'd been saving for Grandpa Ed. He was still at the grill serving up franks and beans. "So, do you attend club meetings during the school year?" she asked.

I supposed I would, even though Grandpa Ed and I hadn't exactly discussed it. "Yeah. I mean, I guess so. I just became a member." Grandpa Ed had paid for my membership as part of my birthday present.

"Us, too. My family moved to Tacoma this summer."

People actually move to Tacoma? I thought, stuffing a spoonful of beans into my mouth. Everyone I knew had always just lived there, like me. "Why'd your family move?"

"My mom got a professor job at University of Washington–Tacoma. She's a marine biologist."

How had this girl gotten so lucky? To have *two* scientist parents! I'd learned on the dig that her dad was an archaeologist.

"So, where do you go to school?" she asked as I took a big bite of hot dog.

"Eastmont Middle, as of next week," I said through my food-filled mouth.

"No way! Me too!"

I coughed up a chunk I'd accidentally inhaled.

"Dad, guess what? Brendan and I are going to be at the same school!"

"Is that so?" Her dad sat in the chair on the other side of her. "That's great. You know, Brendan, you could do me a huge favor."

I was still coughing. "Okay," I said hoarsely, trying to get all my food going in the right direction.

"This will be Morgan's first experience with public school."

"Dad!" Morgan looked as embarrassed as if her dad

had told me she wet the bed. But if he noticed, it didn't stop him from going on.

"And we just moved here from Florida. Morgan's mom and I would feel so much better if there was someone she already knows looking out for her there."

Morgan huffed. "I don't need anyone to look out for me."

I glanced back and forth between them, feeling caught. Her dad waited for my answer.

Morgan smiled suddenly and her face lit up. Literally. The sun reflected off her braces. The plastic spacers had glitter in them. "I don't need anyone to look out for me, but . . . we could be friends." Her voice went up and down on *friends*, like a shrug. Her eyes had gone all googly and she grinned like a clown.

"Uh . . . sure." *What was I saying?* I had just committed to being friends with a girl I barely knew. The words had slipped out before I'd really taken the time to calculate their mass.

So she knew about mineral habits and epochs and finding gigantic crystal clusters. These things were interesting to me, but not so much to my buddies at school. I didn't need a girl trailing me around Eastmont talking loudly about the prehistoric formation of basalt as if it were as exciting as baseball. A girl who used words like *boy-try*—whatever she'd called the hematite—and *Oligocene*. A girl who had glitter in her braces! The guys would totally hassle me!

But I'd said okay. That meant now I'd have to do it. If Tae Kwon Do had taught me anything, it was the importance of integrity, which means keeping one's word.

Morgan grabbed her dad's wrist. "It's a sign, Dad—that I met Brendan before school started. I told you everything would work out!"

If this was a sign, it wasn't a good one. I imagined Khalfani's round lightbulb head. My best friend was already laughing at me.

CHAPTER 4

The next morning, Grandpa Ed made pancakes on his griddle and served them with warm strawberry sauce. I stayed in our tent as long as I could, packing up all my stuff; then I ate fast and slipped away with P.J. for a final walk through the woods. I almost avoided having to talk to Morgan, but she caught me as we were climbing into the truck. "See you at school Tuesday," she said.

"Yeah. See ya."

Grandpa Ed started up the truck. It roared before settling into a low rumble. Morgan looked as if she was waiting for me to say something else, but my mind was as blank as the pages of my new sixth-grade science notebook.

"In case you were wondering why I've never been to public school, I've always been homeschooled."

I hadn't been, but that explained some things. Like

why she talked to adults as if she were one of them. And why she knew so much. And why, honestly, she was so nerdy. The one homeschool kid I'd met at Tae Kwon Do was the same way.

I waited for Grandpa Ed to say it was time to go, but he just sat there humming and tapping the steering wheel with his thumbs, as if he weren't listening.

"I'm glad you liked the hematite I gave you," Morgan said.

I glanced at Grandpa Ed. I hadn't been planning to tell him about that. Didn't want to give him any more fuel for girlfriend jokes. His lips curled into a smile.

"Oh, yeah. Thanks again." The sample was in my backpack. I'd made a note in my *Book of Big Questions* to look up that word Morgan had used to describe it.

She peered around me. "Thanks for leading the expedition, Mr. DeBose. I can't wait to go again!"

"Any time, darlin'. See you around."

"You certainly will." Morgan looked at me. Her eyes sparkled a little too much.

As we drove away, I watched her in the side mirror. She was still waving as we took the first bend headed back down the hill.

———

We got home around noon. Gladys met us at the door. "My milk chocolate is back!" Gladys has been calling me her milk chocolate as long as I can remember. Mom's the color of milk, Dad's the color of chocolate, and I'm the color of them together. "Give me some sugar." Gladys's curly popcorn hair looked newly dyed—orange in the front, black everywhere else.

I pecked her on the cheek. I didn't have to stretch my neck to reach her face anymore. Seemed like I'd grown a couple of inches in just the last few weeks. There had been some other changes, too. Thinking about them made my ears get warm.

"What's a man got to do to get inside?" Grandpa Ed was still on the front steps, holding P.J. by the collar. P.J. barked and strained toward the door.

"Pass inspection," Gladys said, "of my grandson. Now let me see that pretty face." She grabbed my chin and turned my head side to side, peering from behind her pointy glasses. "Better not be any scratches." She eyed Grandpa Ed. "Did Mr. Rock Hudson here take good care of my grandbaby out in that wilderness?" She had given Grandpa Ed the nickname Rock Hudson (some hotshot actor from a long time ago) since he's the president of a rock club.

It was hard to tell whether Grandpa Ed's response would be acidic or neutral. I jumped in. "I'm not a baby anymore, Gladys. I'm starting middle school next week, remember?"

Gladys narrowed her eyes. "I see what you're doing, young man. Let the man speak for himself. He's certainly *old* enough."

"He's my grandson, too, you know. Of course I took good care of him."

"Mama!" Dad spoke from the living room at the top of the stairs. "Let them in already." Football game sounds came from the TV.

"Well, I suppose . . ." Gladys's eyes twinkled. Her face lit up with a smile. "It's good to see you, too, Rock. Come on in." She started up the steps and Grandpa Ed, P.J., and I followed. "Find anything good out there?" she asked.

"A few things," I said, hoisting my backpack higher on my shoulder.

"Well, let's see 'em!" Gladys went and sat next to Dad on the couch.

"Hey, Bren," Dad said, glancing away from the game.

"Hi," I replied, wondering what it would take to get Dad's full attention. A commercial, most likely.

Grandpa Ed took P.J. to the backyard through the sliding glass door in the dining area.

Mom appeared from down the hall. "Hi, sweetie. Did you have fun?" She wrapped her arm around me and kissed the side of my face.

"Forget fun!" Gladys said. "I want to see the booty." She picked up the metal stein she'd recently bought for drinking her Mountain Dew and sipped through the straw.

"Yeah, I had fun," I said to Mom. "Did everything go okay with Einstein?"

Mom nodded. As soon as Gladys was satisfied, I'd go give my anole some top-notch personal attention.

I sat on the love seat and zipped open my backpack's front pocket. I dug around for the largest quartz specimen. I held it up, hoping it would gleam impressively in the sunshine coming through the front window. It looked better than it had back at the campsite.

"That's the biggest diamond I've ever seen in my life!" Gladys exclaimed.

"It's not a diamond. It's a quartz crystal," I said. My family needed some serious education in the field of petrology.

"Oh. Well, it's the largest one of those I've ever seen in my life."

Mom reached for the crystal, and I handed it to her. She turned it in her hands, looking at its surfaces. "This is beautiful, Bren. Sam, did you see?"

Dad looked away from the TV and squinted at my find. He nodded. "Hmm." It was a short sound. The sound Gladys sometimes made when she fell asleep sitting up. "Is there more?"

The ground collapsed inside me. All the work I'd done—first to find the crystal, and then to convince myself it was a good one—vanished into the sinkhole.

I reached into my pack. "I've got a few more in—"

Dad jumped up and hollered at the screen. "Run it! Run it! Run it! Yesssss!"

But nothing worth getting too excited about, I thought, leaving the fragments where they were.

Mom handed me the crystal. "It's beautiful, honey." I dropped the mineral back into the pouch and zipped it shut.

Grandpa Ed came back inside without P.J. "When's lunch? I'm starving!" He slapped his hands and rubbed them together. "Fresh mountain air makes a man hungry, eh, Brendan?"

Lately, it seemed I'd been famished every moment of the day, but suddenly I had no appetite. My heart felt like a big dirt clod. And it had just been smashed to smithereens.

CHAPTER 5

The first day of school, I was up and ready to go an hour early, which gave me time to do some online research. I wanted to make sure I knew what botryoidal meant before I saw Morgan again. I quickly discovered that a habit, when referring to minerals, just means the shape a mineral takes as a result of its crystalline structure. A botryoidal habit is one that looks like bunches of grapes, which *does* accurately describe my piece of kidney ore.

I'd put my newest acquisition on the shelf with my Ellensburg Blue, where I kept my entire collection of fourteen specimens. Morgan might have been a little too excited, but still, it had been cool of her to give me the hematite. I'd tossed all the quartz pieces into my garbage can the night we'd returned from the dig. They were like the fish Grampa Clem and I would throw back into the bay. Too puny to keep.

I checked and recorded Einstein's tank temperatures and misted the tank. "See you after school, boy." I grabbed my backpack, turned out my bedroom light, and went to find my parents. They were in the kitchen. Dad was gathering up the garbage to take it to the curb, and Mom was on the phone.

"You sure you don't want me to take you on my way to work?" Dad had suggested that he walk me into school wearing his uniform. "Be a sure way to keep the older kids from pushing you around."

Be a sure way to get a whole lot of the wrong kind of attention, I thought. "Nah. I'll be all right. Thanks, though."

Mom hung up the phone. "Ready to see how much you've grown, Boo?"

I nodded. It was our first-day-of-school tradition. I'd stand against the inside of the kitchen doorjamb and Mom would mark my height.

"I'm not sure *I'm* ready," Mom said, smiling.

I backed up against the wall and looked straight ahead. Mom's eyes were no longer level with mine. They were a little lower. The pencil scraped back and forth across my head. I stepped away and Dad measured. "Five-five and a half," he announced.

Mom gasped. "You've passed me by half an inch!" Her green eyes watered. Mom wasn't going to cry, was she? She isn't usually a crier.

Dad pounded me on the back. "Way to go, buddy! Three inches since last year."

I looked at the marks. It was crazy to see how much I'd grown in the past few years. Even crazier to think I might one day be as tall as Dad.

Mom had turned away to get something from the counter. When she turned back, her eyes looked normal again. She handed me a stiff notebook with a black and white marbled cover and a black binding. It said COMPOSITION on the front and had lines for the user's name, school, and grade.

"I know you were keeping a question notebook this summer," Mom said. "I thought you might like to have a new notebook for starting middle school. A place to write down things you're thinking about."

"You mean, like a *journal?*" I felt my face scrunch up. Weren't journals for girls?

Dad spoke up. "You could think of it as a log, like officers keep when they're on duty."

"Or like scientists keep when they're doing research," Mom said. "It could be your own private lab book—a place to record your observations about being in the sixth grade."

A scientific log. Now, that was more like it. I could already see the title page: *Inquiries and Investigations of a Sixth-Grade Scientist: A Log by Brendan S. Buckley.*

"Thanks, Mom." I put the logbook in my backpack and we all went down to the garage.

"Remember to show respect to your new teachers," Dad said, giving me a sideways hug. He gripped my head with his large palm.

"Yes, sir."

He kissed Mom. "See you tonight—after my first class. Wish me luck."

"Should we measure you, too?" Mom smiled and kissed him again. "And you don't need any luck. You'll do great."

Mom and I got in her car and she drove me to school. It was just a couple of minutes' ride. After today, I'd be walking—at least until I could save up enough allowance money to buy a new bike. My old one had been stolen one day this summer when I'd left it in the bushes at a bus stop. I'd been secretly going to see Grandpa Ed. It had been a stupid thing to do. Not visiting Grandpa Ed—just the way I went about it. I had learned the hard way that keeping secrets like that from my parents didn't pay.

Mom pulled in to the turnaround and stopped near the front of the school, in line with several other cars dropping kids off. "First day of middle school. My boo is truly growing up." She was getting mushy on me again. I had to make my escape quick, before she planted her lips on my face.

"See you later, Mom." I hopped out of the car.

Mom leaned over and looked out the passenger door. "See you right here after school. Got it?"

"Got it." I shut the door firmly and turned toward the building. I heard the automatic window roll down.

"Love you!" she called out.

"Me too!" I yelled over my shoulder.

A few steps later, I turned for real and waved. The car hadn't moved, of course. She blew me a kiss. We grinned at each other. I love my mom. I just didn't want her to give me a big smooch in front of a bunch of other kids on my first day of middle school.

I walked toward the entrance, gripping the straps on my backpack. Khal had told me he'd heard of sixth graders getting shoved into lockers, or having their underwear ripped off and hung in the bushes. Would I get stuffed into a locker or be tackled for my underpants?

Dozens of kids milled around on the sidewalk and playing field. No one else seemed in a hurry to get inside, but I wanted to go say hi to Mr. Hammond. My fifth-grade and favorite teacher of all time had taken an open science position at Eastmont, so he was moving from grade school to middle school, same as us. Knowing Mr. H was somewhere in this big sprawling building helped me feel a little less nervous.

A blur came at me from the side. Was someone after me already?

I shouted and put up my hands in a *mak-gee*—a block. After two years of practicing almost every day, Tae Kwon Do moves came as naturally to me as riding my bike.

The blur rammed into me. Khalfani wrapped his arm around my neck and pulled me into his chest. "Hey, man! Where you been? Oscar and I been waiting ten minutes already." We pretended to spar for a second; then he tugged me in the direction of the far side of the building. Oscar and Marcus stood on the other side of the chain-link fence, throwing a football back and forth.

I was glad I wasn't being led to a bathroom stall to have my head flushed in a toilet, but I didn't feel like playing ball right then. "Wait a sec." I stopped and Khal let go. "I was headed in to say hi to Mr. H."

"Who?"

"Mr. Hammond. Our science teacher."

Khal rolled his eyes. "Aw, man. That can wait. Come on, we need you to play two-on-two!"

A girl's voice came from behind. "Brendan! Brendan!" I didn't need to look to know who it was. Even though my Tae Kwon Do integrity meter told me I shouldn't, I started walking toward the field. Quickly.

Khal caught up. "Did you become a celebrity recently or something? Because you've got a girl chasing you."

I didn't stop. "Oscar and Marcus are waiting, remember?"

"Too late," Khal said.

Morgan rushed up, her eyes gleaming. "Hi, Brendan! Isn't this so exciting? Our first day of middle school! I was hoping I'd see you outside, so we could walk in together. It's much nicer to walk into a new place with someone you know. Don't you think?"

She was talking a mile a millisecond. "Sure," I said. I didn't want to be mean, but I already *had* friends to walk into school with.

Morgan held out her hand to Khalfani. "Hi, I'm Morgan. What's your name?"

Khal scrunched his face. "Morgan? As in Morgan Freeman? Isn't that a boy's name?"

"Actually, it's unisex. And how do you know I'm not named after Morgan Freeman? He's an extraordinary actor."

"Extraordinary?" Khal's eyes slid over to meet mine.

"This is Khalfani. My best friend," I said, so she would know the position was already taken.

"It's a pleasure to meet you, Khalfani." Morgan held out her hand again. If she ever took up Tae Kwon Do she wouldn't have any problem with tenet number three, *in nae.* Perseverance. "What's the origin of your name? It's beautiful."

"*Beautiful?*" Khal's face scrunched even more. He looked at Morgan as if she had just dropped in from outer space.

"I mean, it's—it's very n-nice," Morgan stammered. Her cheeks turned pink.

I felt kind of bad for her, but she had brought this on herself. Calling a boy's name beautiful was never a good idea.

"It's Swahili." Khalfani puffed out his chest and lifted his chin. Morgan and I still stood taller than him. "It means 'destined to lead.' But that doesn't mean I want *everyone* to follow me." He grabbed my arm and pulled me along.

The skin between Morgan's eyebrows crinkled. I saw the hurt look in her eyes, but I turned and walked away before that look could get to me and make me do something I'd regret.

"Who was *that?*" Khal asked.

I had a feeling she was still there, watching us walk away—watching me do something that I knew was cold. But didn't *she* know she was embarrassing me in front of my best friend? Maybe this way, she'd get the message.

"Just a girl from my rock club." I wasn't about to tell him that I'd spent a night in the woods with her. Or that I'd promised to hang around with her at school.

"Why was she talking to you like you're her best friend?"

I shrugged and kept walking, but I felt like a slug trailing slime. I started to run. When I got to the fence, I glanced back. She was gone.

———

When we got to homeroom, Morgan wasn't there. My shoulders relaxed with relief. I wasn't trying to be mean. It was just that Morgan was like this wiry, bouncy, talking paper clip. And I was a giant magnet. I didn't want a talking paper clip stuck to my backside my whole first year of middle school. Hopefully she'd find some *girls* to be friends with and wouldn't want to be around me so much. Problem solved.

The final bell rang and Ms. Manley called us to attention. "Okay, listen up. You are currently in Room 6E. Look at your class schedule and make sure you're in the right place. This is where you'll come at the start of each day for roll call and advisory. We'll work on the skills you need to make the best possible transition to the new and exciting world of middle school." She didn't sound too excited. "If you're in pre-algebra, you'll stay with me for first period as well. Got it?"

Several people nodded, including me. This woman was serious.

Khal smacked his gum. The teacher eyed him, lifted the garbage can, and walked to our row. She didn't say anything—just held the can in front of Khal's face. Her biceps were nearly as big as Dad's. Khal spit his gum out.

While she was taking roll, the door opened. I expected it to be an adult with some kind of message, but it wasn't. It was a short kid with a buzz cut wearing camouflage pants, a brown T-shirt, and a military dog tag around his neck. His skin was brown, but he didn't look black, exactly. His eyes were shaped like footballs and were black as coal.

Behind him was Morgan. The rims of her eyes looked pink and watery, and her face was splotchy.

I shriveled like an ant under a magnifying glass in the sun.

"She was lost," the boy announced, "but I found her." He led her to Ms. Manley's desk.

"Thank you, Mister . . ." Ms. Manley waited for the boy to tell her his name.

"Del Santos. Dwight David!" The boy threw back his shoulders, clicked his heels, and saluted the class. Some of the kids laughed. Was he joking? Or did he really think school was like the army? Ms. Manley sure enough could've been a drill sergeant.

"Thank you, Mr. Del Santos. Have a seat."

The boy marched to an empty chair, spun a one-eighty, did another salute, and sat. Definitely joking. More kids laughed, including Khal and me. Ms. Manley gave the class a sharp look and we all shut our mouths. She turned to Morgan. "And you are?"

"Morgan," she said quietly. She pointed to her name on Ms. Manley's list.

"Thank you, Miss Belcher."

"*Belcher?*" Khalfani practically shouted.

Cordé Wilkins, who'd been known throughout our elementary school for his crazy-loud burps, must have seen his chance to establish a reputation at Eastmont. He let out the longest, juiciest belch I'd ever heard.

"Ewwww!" Both girls *and* boys were grossed out.

Khal waved his hand in front of his nose. "Man, Cordé! What'd you have for breakfast? Chili dogs?"

When people laughed this time, I bit the side of my cheek. Morgan had turned about as pink as a flamingo.

"That's enough!" Ms. Manley commanded. She glared at Cordé. "Young man, I'm confident you don't want to spend the first hour of your first day of middle school in the principal's office. Am I right?"

Cordé looked genuinely scared. I didn't blame him. Ms. Manley wasn't taking any mess.

Welcome to middle school.

CHAPTER 6

Turned out Morgan and I not only shared the same homeroom, we also had our first two classes together—pre-algebra and computer keyboarding—*and* we were locker neighbors. She *would* have to have a last name that started with B. The first time I saw her getting things out of the locker next to mine, I hung back, waiting for her to leave.

By the time third-period science rolled around and I still hadn't talked to Morgan, I felt like a moldy sandwich—the guilt was eating at me like a fungus on bread. I tried to forget about it as I joked around with Khal on the way to Mr. Hammond's class. Khal and I had gone to different elementary schools—we'd met at Tae Kwon Do—so he didn't know Mr. H. "You're really going to like him. His two favorite foods are chocolate and Coke."

My arms swung free and easy. I had my brand-new

spiral-bound science notebook in my hand. And I was walking toward my favorite teacher's class for my favorite subject with my best friend. Life couldn't get any better than this.

The science room door was closed. Black paper covered the window. A sign on the glass said LABORATORY OF MAD SCIENTIST HAMMOND. ENTER AT YOUR OWN RISK! A hand-drawn lightning bolt was electrocuting a stick-figure person—some poor sixth grader who hadn't taken the proper precautions.

Inside, several kids sat in pairs behind long tables, all facing the counter and whiteboard at the front of the room. Mr. Hammond had his back to the door, talking to someone. I was dying to talk to Mr. H, too, but I'm not the kind of person who goes up to people when they're already speaking with someone else. Gladys would, but not me.

Khal and I sat at an empty table. I opened my notebook, which was full of blank pages just waiting to be filled with observations, data, and sources. Tables, charts, and graphs. Questions, hypotheses, and conclusions.

I wrote my name and "Mr. Hammond—3rd Period Science" on the first page. I had just started to write "Lab Notebook" when the person Mr. H had been talking to laughed. I already knew whose giggle it was, but I looked anyway. Morgan. A little bug of jealousy crawled up my neck. *Don't be stupid*, I thought. *Mr. Hammond was your teacher for a whole year. She just met him today.*

Morgan looked a lot happier than she had all morning. She had a big, goofy smile on her face. She came out from behind the counter and sat in the first row next to Aadesh Kapur, who everyone called Dash, because it sounded sort of like the second half of his first name but also because he had been the fastest kid in the fifth grade. He was also the brainiest. He and Morgan would get along well.

The bell rang and a few more kids rushed in. Without saying a word, Mr. Hammond pulled out a green balloon and began blowing it up. He tied it off, then blew up a red one. It grew bigger and bigger.

"Pop," Jaivier Brown said, breaking the tense silence. A couple of girls giggled. I sat forward in my chair, eager to see what Mr. H would do next.

"Morgan, would you assist me, please?"

The jealousy bug wormed around inside my chest.

Morgan got that goofy smile on her face again and went to the front.

"I need one more assistant. Brendan . . ."

The jolt of hearing my name made my face tingle and my heart race. I jumped up and hurried forward like a contestant on Gladys's favorite game show, *The Price Is Right*.

Mr. H handed me the green balloon, to which he'd tied a string. He gave the red balloon, also on a string, to Morgan. "If you would be so kind as to rub these latex spheres on your heads." He motioned to the balloons.

I hesitated. Rub a balloon on my head? I knew what would happen if I did that. I'd have one giant Afro. But for Mr. H, I'd do it.

We both started rubbing. *Scritch, scritch, scritch.* Morgan's hair jumped up and stuck to the balloon. I could feel the static electricity building. By the time this was over, I would look like the electrocuted stick figure on Mr. H's sign.

"Now," Mr. Hammond said, "hold your balloons by the strings and bring them near each other."

I didn't want to have to get too close to Morgan—especially in front of the whole class—but again, for Mr. H and for the sake of science, I went along. We brought our balloons together. They separated, as if under a magic spell. Of course, it wasn't magic. Just two negatively charged balloons repelling each other.

Morgan leaned in and whispered, "Same charges repel."

"Yeah. I know," I whispered back.

"Now," Mr. H said again, "watch this." He put a piece of paper between the balloons. *Swup.* They glommed together.

"Ooo, they're kissing!" Cordé shouted out. I felt my face getting warm.

Mr. H pulled out the paper and the balloons moved away from each other. "Uh-oh. Lovers' quarrel," Javier said. More giggles.

"Can we get them to make up somehow?" Mr.

Hammond asked. Did he have to play into all this mushy stuff? It was bad enough we had to talk about it in health.

Lauren Dweck spoke up. "Use the paper again."

Mr. H slipped the paper between the balloons and they went right back to sucking face.

"Can anyone give me a scientific explanation for what we're witnessing here?"

Morgan jumped in so fast I didn't have a chance. "The balloons picked up electrons from our hair, giving them an overall negative charge. Like charges repel; therefore the balloons moved away from each other."

"Very good. And now?" Mr. H asked, looking down at the stuck-together balloons.

"It looks to me like Brendan's and Morgan's balloons are *attracted* to each other!" Cordé said. Some of the guys laughed, including Kahl. I scowled at my best friend out of the corner of my eye. He'd better watch it.

"Actually," I said, "they're attracted to the paper, which has a positive charge. *Not* to each other."

"That's right, Brendan," Mr. H said. "Opposite charges attract. Same charges repel. Hopefully, this was just a review for everyone, but if you didn't know it before, you should learn it now. Let's give our volunteers a round of applause."

Everyone clapped. I kept my eyes down and returned to my seat. Khal nudged my arm. I ignored him.

Mr. Hammond went on to talk about how electrons

move around and that's where electricity comes from. I had to write like lightning, but I got it all down. By the time he was done, I felt all charged up, like a big rain cloud.

"Now, I have a very important announcement to make," Mr. H said. "This year, we have the opportunity to participate in an online science competition for middle school students. The theme is 'Making the World Better.'"

A science competition! *Yes!* I buzzed from head to toe.

"There are divisions for sixth-, seventh-, and eighth-grade teams, and each team must consist of at least two people. . . ."

I bumped Khal's elbow with mine.

"Regional finalists will be chosen from across the United States."

Kids from all over the country? This was huge!

"The winning team will receive a nice sum of money—"

"Ka-*ching*," Khal whispered. "Now we're talking."

"—to enhance their school's science program."

Khal groaned in disappointment.

"They will also get to travel to an institute of higher learning to work with top scientists in the field of their project."

Whoa. Now, *that* would be cool!

Mr. H smiled. "I believe we have some finalist

potential in this room." His eyes dared us to rise to the challenge. "Who knows? Maybe even a first-place team."

I grinned. Winning the top prize in a national science competition . . . No touchdown, no matter how impressive, could even come *near* that.

Log Entry—Tuesday, September 4

I'm officially an Eastmont Eagle! I made it through my first day, no problem. No wedgies, no having my pants ripped off, no getting eaten alive like one of Einstein's pinhead crickets. The older kids didn't even seem to notice we were there.

I like switching teachers for every class. It's like we're in high school. And they treat us like we're older, too. We're going to have a lot more homework. I've never heard the word <u>responsible</u> used so much in one day.

Observation: Girls in middle school smell a lot more perfume-y than girls in elementary.

Chapter 7

That Friday I was still researching ideas for science projects. Mr. Hammond had given us two weeks to come up
with our proposals. He would pair us up based on common interest and leave it to us to choose between our
two proposals or come up with a third idea. Khalfani and
I had agreed: No matter what, we would be partners.

I sat at my computer, rubbing my almost-pinky-sized
quartz between my fingers. I'd discovered it and a few of
the other fragments next to a pile of folded laundry on
my desk when I'd gotten home from the first day of
school. Mom had probably seen them in my garbage can
and couldn't just leave them there. *Oh well*, I'd thought.
I'll keep them for now. I could replace them with bigger
ones later.

I turned my attention back to my assignment. I
wanted my experiment to be focused on something *big*,

something that really mattered. I'd know I'd found the right project idea when I got the Jitters—that tingling, twitching, electrical-storm feeling in my body that came on whenever I had a whole bunch of questions about something.

Another half hour of browsing the Internet passed, and I still hadn't come up with a single idea—nothing that lit the flame in my Bunsen burner, anyway.

I went to find Dad. Maybe he'd play a few rounds of Mario vs. Donkey Kong 2 with me. I'd already finished my homework from that day, spent some time observing Einstein, and practiced my *hyung* for Tae Kwon Do. I needed to come up with a proposal, and playing video games sometimes sparked good ideas in my brain.

Hey . . . maybe there was a science experiment in *that*. If I researched the connection between playing video games and getting good ideas, I'd have to play Mario hundreds, maybe even thousands, of times. That wouldn't be too bad—for the sake of science, of course.

Dad sat at his desk in the basement, hunched over a book. He'd turned an unfinished side room into his study. It was dark everywhere except for the small desk lamp and the glow of the computer's wiggly neon screen saver that reminded me of Proterozoic amoebas swimming around in dark, uninhabited ocean waters.

I knocked on the hollow wooden door to get his attention. He glanced my way but went right back to his book. His square jaw worked a piece of gum. "Hey, buddy, what's up?"

"Do you want to play Nintendo?"

"Done with your homework already?"

"Yeah."

"Teachers go easy this first week?"

"Actually, they gave us a ton of work. I think they wanted to make sure we know we're not in elementary school anymore."

"Mmm." Dad wrote on a yellow legal pad next to his book.

"So, do you want to play?"

"Can't right now. My ton of work is still a ton." He turned to the computer and opened a blank document. "Later. Promise."

If Dad said *Promise*, I knew he was good for it. Problem was, when was later? He'd been using that word so often in the last couple of weeks I could have charted its frequency on a line graph.

By nine o'clock, when Dad still hadn't appeared, I got ready for bed, said good night to Mom, and gave Einstein's tank one last squirt. Einstein crawled out from the ivy along one of the jungle vines I'd attached to the side of the tank. I stared into his black dot of an eye, which looked like a blob of extra ink from a ballpoint pen. It sat in the center of a round ridge of skin like a bull's-eye. The skin under his eye was tinged light blue. I recorded these things in the *Other Observations* section of my green notebook. In the *Questions* section I wrote, "Do all green anoles have a patch of light blue under their eyes? Why?"

Einstein lapped at water droplets on an overhanging leaf, then darted into the shadows.

"Good night, boy."

A glint from the shelf caught my eye. I put down my notebook and picked up my specimen of slate. I'd found it this summer and decided it would be for Grampa Clem, because it was black and thin like he was, but also because it was sedimentary—rock that had been formed under pressure, just like black people in the United States.

I sat on my bed, loosely grasping the rock. It was barely heavier than a penny. Not at all like the solid presence of Grampa Clem as we sat on the bench outside his and Gladys's apartment, talking about how I wanted to be a scientist when I grew up. He had told me about George Washington Carver—"that man knew about a whole lot more than just peanuts"—and Vivien Thomas, "a black man who taught the nation's top heart surgeons how to do their jobs, back when a black man couldn't even urinate in the same spot as a white man."

So you go on and be a scientist, Grampa Clem had said that day on the bench. *You'd be joining a long line of our people who made life-changing discoveries. Made this world a better place, they did.* He put his hand on my knee. *And you'll make it better yet.*

I still didn't have a proposal for the science competition, but I went to sleep with Grampa Clem's voice in my ears and a little reminder of him in my hand.

CHAPTER 8

At Oscar's house that weekend, Khal, Oscar, and I loaded up our Super Soakers and ran around Oscar's house trying to drench each other. It was a warm day, but not exactly hot. I never stopped moving, because when I did I got goose bumps the size of geodes. Still, I couldn't shake Khalfani. He'd blasted me pretty good a few times.

When Khal went for a refill, I pulled Oscar into a bush at the opposite side of his house from the spigot. Oscar's T-shirt was soaked and water dripped from his hair and face. It was hard to tell what was from the water guns and what was sweat, but clearly, Khal was dominating us both. It was time to team up.

"We'll ambush him," I said. "You go around back. I'll go around front. As soon as the water is off, attack!" We had a rule that you couldn't squirt someone in the middle of a refill.

Oscar nodded. We crept from our hiding place, nozzles pointed up. I had barely gotten around the corner of the house when I heard Oscar yelling. His voice was getting louder. "Ahhhhhh!"

I looked back just in time to see him ram into me. We both fell to the ground. Khal stood over us, pumping his soaker mercilessly.

I jumped up and stood my ground, shooting at Khal even as a spray of water pummeled my face and chest. When Oscar finally got to his feet, it was two against one, but Khal wouldn't back down. We all just kept screaming and pumping until our soakers were empty.

When the water was gone, we dropped our guns to our sides and looked at each other. "I think we're all dead," Oscar said. We laughed then.

"What I am is *hungry*," Khal said. "You got something we can eat?"

"Cheese crunchies," Oscar said with a shrug.

"Sounds good to me," Khal said. We followed Oscar inside, took off our shoes, and headed to his bedroom, which was a total disaster zone. Oscar got us each a towel.

I was glad Mom had made me bring along some extra clothes when she saw me leaving the house with my water gun. I stripped off my wet pants, then pushed aside an empty Doritos bag, a bunch of game discs, and an army of Pokémon figures so I could sit on the bed to pull on my dry ones. Khal borrowed some of Oscar's clothes. They were kind of baggy, but they worked.

We went to the kitchen and sat at the table while Oscar got the bag of cheese puffs and some Cokes from the fridge. "Thanks," I said.

Khal already had his pop can open and was chugging it down. "Yeah, thanks," he said, coming up for air. He swiped at his lips with the back of his hand. "I needed that."

"Do either of you have any ideas for the science competition yet?" I asked.

Khal let out a big belch. "Maybe we could research the connection between carbonation and burping."

"What is there to research?" I asked. "You drink a carbonated beverage and then you burp."

"Yeah, but how soon after you start drinking and at what rate? And do some sodas make you burp more than others?" Khal raised his eyebrows, like, *Huh? What about that?* He tipped back his can and drank some more.

"Sounds like a good idea to me," Oscar said. "You'd get to drink lots of pop for your research."

"Exactly." Khal grinned. "I could get Cordé Wilkins to be my partner."

"Or your subject," I said. We all laughed. "Hey, I thought *we* were going to be partners."

"Just joking." Khal popped a cheese crunchy in his mouth. "So, what do you propose we do, Mr. Science?"

"I don't know yet," I said.

"Brendan 'Ask a Million Questions' Buckley doesn't have a research idea? I thought you'd be halfway done with our experiment by now."

Oscar's mom came in then, carrying Oscar's baby brother, William. I don't care what people say. Babies are not really that cute. The kid reminded me of a cooked raisin—plump and wrinkled at the same time. His black hair went in all directions, including a patch on top that stood straight up. I wasn't sure yet what I thought about us getting a baby at our house. Sometime around my birthday, Mom and Dad had started discussing the idea of adopting one. I'd found out this past summer that Mom can't have any more babies, and that she'd almost died having me.

"Hello, boys," Mrs. Hernandez said. "*Oscar, no te olvides de nuestro acuerdo. ¿Tu cuarto?*"

"I know. I'll clean it up as soon as my friends leave." He looked at us. "My room." I could never keep my room the way Oscar did—not in Detective Buckley's house. Not that I wanted to, anyway. I liked being able to find things.

William started to squirm in Mrs. Hernandez's arms. The corners of his lips turned down and his face turned red. I braced myself for some loud crying, but the squishy, juicy sound that came out didn't erupt from his mouth.

"Ewww!" Khal and I said at once.

"You stinker!" Oscar's mom said.

Stinker was right. I could smell the results of William's efforts from where I sat at the table.

"*Acabo de cambiar tu pañal.*"

"She just changed his diaper," Oscar whispered.

Mrs. Hernandez shook her head. "If only your poops were made of gold!"

"My brother is like a poop machine," Oscar said when his mom had left the kitchen. "I don't know how a little baby can make so much of the stuff."

That was when it hit me. An idea for the science competition! A *big* idea! Possibly even a national science competition award—*winning* idea!

I had read about how scientists are looking into more and more efficient ways to use cow manure as fuel. It's a completely renewable resource, and burning the methane it produces puts a whole lot less junk into the atmosphere than coal.

But what about human waste? Wasn't that a renewable resource, as well? And as William could demonstrate, a superabundant one at that!

I turned to Oscar. "Can I get on the Internet?"

"Sure." We went back to his room. Oscar pushed the pile of magic-trick paraphernalia from his chair and plucked off the dirty underwear hanging over the back. "Here you go."

I removed the soccer shirt covering the computer screen, opened his web browser, and typed in "poop and energy."

"Poop and *energy?*" Khal said. I didn't have to turn around to know he was making a disgusted face.

One million two hundred thirty thousand results came back. I was definitely on to something.

"I think I've got an idea for the science contest," I said.

Khal crossed his arms. "You think I'm going to be your partner if you're messing around with poop? Forget that!"

"What kind of an experiment would you do on poop?" Oscar asked.

"More importantly, *why* would you do an experiment on poop?" Khal asked.

I scanned the list for science fair ideas, ignoring Khal. "I don't know exactly, but I know burning cow dung creates energy. What about other forms of waste? What about *human* waste? There's got to be some kind of experiment in that."

"Uh-uh," Khal said. "No one's going to catch *me* making energy logs out of doo-doo."

I read some of the article titles out loud. "Listen to this: 'Poop Power: Sewage Turned into Electricity.' . . . 'Pet Poop: The Energy of Tomorrow?'" I pointed to the screen. "Look, this one's on a website called Poop Report.com!"

We all laughed at that. Even Khal.

There was one article called "The Biogas Machine: Turning Poop (Yes, Poop) into Energy." I clicked on it.

I read about a "biodigester"—a way to trap methane from manure and use it as fuel. There was even a YouTube video showing a guy cooking hash browns over a flame created with the methane from his digester. "Check that out!" I said. "Come on, Khal. We could make one of those digester things. It'd be so cool."

"It'd be so *nasty*, is what it'd be. My stepmom made me empty Dori's diaper pail once. I thought I was going to puke! My nostrils were *traumatized*, man."

"How old is Dori now? Four?" I said. "Get over it already!"

"Baby poop *is* pretty gross," Oscar said.

"I thought we agreed," I said. "Partners, no matter what."

"I didn't know you were going to be grilling food over poop."

"You don't grill it over the poop. The poop just provides the gas to make the flame over which you *could* grill food if you wanted to."

"Whatever. Maybe if I was playing a joke on my sister, but not for homework. No way. Do you realize the kinds of names we'd get called?" Khal picked up Oscar's football and spun it in the air. "Now I know where they get the *mad* in *mad scientist*."

I could tell the conversation was closed as far as Khal was concerned, but I was no less determined to pursue my idea.

"How about you, Oscar?" I looked at my other friend.

"You want to join me in some serious scientific research that could help save the planet?"

"Uh . . ." Oscar glanced at Khal. "I was kind of thinking about doing something with Pop Rocks."

"Your choice. But this is going to be *good*. I can feel it." I stuffed my wet clothes into my backpack. "I'll see you guys later. I've got a proposal to write."

Log Entry—Thursday, September 13

Went to my first official rock club meeting as a member tonight. Morgan showed off her amethyst-tinged crystal cluster. She asked what I'm proposing for the science competition. No way was I going to share that top-secret information! Told her I wasn't sure, even though I knew I wasn't practicing complete *yom chi*, integrity. But she shouldn't be so nosy.

As far as sixth grade goes, so far, so good. Science, of course, is my favorite class. The other day, we popped balloons with just magnifying glasses and the sun's rays! I know Mr. H is really going to like my proposal, since it deals with a totally underused energy source: biomass. In class, we've been talking about energy from heat, light, and motion.

Speaking of motion, that kid Dwight David never stops moving. He's like a toy with no Off switch. He's really distracting. He dropped a rubber band onto Morgan's desk in World Civilizations and yelled, "Dead worm!" Morgan giggled and handed it back to him. Mrs. Simmons didn't think it was so funny. Neither did I.

CHAPTER 9

A week and a half after I got my idea at Oscar's house, we sat in science class waiting to hear who our partners would be for the competition. Khal had proposed something related to projectiles, so it was unlikely we'd get put together, even though I'd dropped lots of hints to Mr. Hammond that Khal and I would make a super team. I was 99.9 percent sure I'd get paired with Aadesh. Clearly, Mr. H wanted to win the money. He knew Aadesh was a brain. Together, we'd be unstoppable!

"Khalfani Jones and Dwight David Del Santos," Mr. Hammond announced.

"Dang," Khal said under his breath. "That kid's a complete knucklehead."

"Too bad," I whispered, "but you had your chance to work with a serious scientist."

Khal crossed his arms and sank lower in his chair.

"Brendan Buckley . . ."

My ears perked up.

"And Morgan Belcher."

Khal sputtered like a waterlogged engine.

Morgan scowled in our direction.

I shook my head quickly and hitched my thumb toward Khal to let her know it wasn't me who'd made the sound.

Mr. Hammond continued. "You both had great ideas for alternative energy projects and I know together you'll come up with something stellar."

Morgan grinned at Mr. H.

I slumped back in my seat. How could my favorite teacher *do* this to me?

———

After class, Morgan accosted Khal and me like a cop going after a couple of criminals. Was I still a criminal in Morgan's eyes? After the first day of school, she hadn't seemed to want to talk to me as much, just hi and bye if we ran into each other at our lockers. I'd avoided her at the rock club meeting by sitting between Grandpa Ed and one of his buddies.

My conscience poked me every once in a while, trying to get me to do something about it, but really, what was there to do? Anyway, I'd seen her talking to some girls here and there—Shyla-Ann Thompson and Lauren Dweck, among others.

"Hey, Liver," Khal said.

Morgan's nose wrinkled and her eyebrows scrunched together.

"As in *organ?*" Khal said. "Get it? Morgan. Organ." Khal laughed. I rolled my eyes.

"Oh." Morgan let out a little laugh.

"Have fun playing with your cow doo-doo," he said.

Morgan's nose wrinkled again.

"You coming?" Khal asked, starting toward the cafeteria.

I glanced back and forth between him and Morgan, who hadn't moved and seemed intent on talking to me. "Uh . . . I'll be there in a few minutes."

Dwight David zoomed by and held up his hand to slap Khal a high five. Khal didn't leave him hanging, but I could tell he wasn't exactly fired up.

"Okay, so you acted like a protozoa toward me on the first day of school," Morgan said.

I stood there feeling dumb. I could try to apologize, but I'd probably just make things worse. Let her believe what she wanted. I knew I wasn't as awful as she seemed to think I was. I cleared my throat.

"And you haven't treated me much better since then, not even at the club meeting, even though you *said* you wanted to be my friend when we were on the dig."

My ears got warm. I looked at my shoelaces. Morgan seemed like an okay girl. But that was the problem. She was a *girl*. None of my buddies hung out with girls. And her mouth just never stopped moving! Yes, Morgan and I had some common interests. But did that mean I had to like her?

No. *But you said you would be her friend.*

"Sorry," I mumbled.

Morgan shrugged. "It's all right."

I stood there silently, but my brain was screaming *Run!* and my muscles twitched like they might actually do it.

"We could have a do-over," Morgan suggested. "That's what we call it in my family. You know, a fresh start. Whatever you did to mess up, it can't be held against you." She held out her hand. "So, what do you say? Do-over?"

I *wanted* to say I hadn't messed up. Didn't she know it wasn't cool for a guy to hang around with a smart, nerdy girl? I glanced around. Only a few other kids were in the hall, and they weren't paying attention to us. I shook her hand quickly and let go.

Morgan grabbed the crook of my arm. "Isn't it fantastic that we get to be partners for this incredible competition?"

I pulled away and started toward my locker. She caught up with me.

"We're going to *win*, Brendan! We'll be the Dynamic Duo!"

I wasn't so sure. Maybe I could still go to Mr. Hammond and ask him to switch me and Lauren Dweck,

Aadesh's partner. Aadesh had proposed a cool-sounding project on artificial intelligence. And Morgan and Lauren seemed to like each other all right. Mr. H could just say he'd rethought the assignments.

"Do you want to come to my house after school to talk about our experiment? What's your interest in alternative fuels? And what was Khalfani talking about back there, anyway? Cow doo-doo? Oh! I know. You want to do something with biomass." Morgan "Mile a Minute" Belcher opened her locker.

I flubbed the combination and had to try again. I couldn't focus with Miss Energy Ball asking so many questions. How would I ever be able to complete the detailed measurements and observations required for my experiment with her talking in my ear?

I dropped my books into my locker and grabbed my red gym bag. As soon as I shut the door, she grabbed my arm again and started walking. "We have so much to discuss. This is going to be great. Great!"

She didn't even know what my idea *was*. "What about what you proposed?" I stopped abruptly in the middle of the hall.

Her hand—thankfully no longer on my arm—waved away my question. "Watching algae grow? Bo-ring! It was my mom's idea, anyway."

I'd come across several articles on algae farmers and harvesters while doing my research on alternative fuels. "Algae has a lot of potential as a future energy source."

"Believe me, I know. My mom's a marine biologist, remember?"

I started walking. Of course I remembered. How could I forget that *both* of her parents were scientists?

Morgan caught up with me again. She was as sticky as a housefly. "Personally, I think cow poop sounds like much more fun." Her eyes sparkled with excitement.

I stopped. Apparently, she was like a fly in more ways than one. "You *do*?"

She nodded like one of the bobbleheads in Oscar's bedroom window. I pulled my chin into my neck. What kind of girl thought cow poop sounded like fun? "You're not grossed out by the idea?"

"Are you kidding? I'm a scientist! Nothing grosses out scientists. Not good ones, anyway." She smiled.

Morgan thought of herself as a scientist, too. We started to walk again, but now my scalp felt tingly, as if I'd been plugged in.

"What are all those patches on your duffel bag?"

I was bringing my gym clothes home for Mom to wash. There might have been some algae growing in the sweaty pair of socks I'd left in my bag all week. "They're from Tae Kwon Do tournaments. Khal and I are purple belts."

"You do Tae Kwon Do? Wow!" Morgan looked at me as if I were wearing a red cape and had a big BB on my chest.

Maybe Morgan Belcher would make an okay partner. I could at least give her a chance.

Log Entry—Tuesday, September 25

Mom and Dad are moving forward with adopting. Today Mom was working on a scrapbook to give to the adoption agency—pictures of our family and descriptions of what we're all like. I asked her to put in a picture of Grampa Clem. He might not be here anymore, but whatever child we get needs to know about him. He's still a part of our family. She agreed.

Mom and Dad say we have to make some decisions about what kind of child we want. They said their only request is that he or she be African American or some mixture that includes African American. That sounds good to me. Mom really wants a girl and she'd like to have a baby, but Dad wants to stay open to a boy and to getting an older child—any age up to seven or eight. Hearing that made me get the jitters. Why would he want to get an older boy when he's already got me? And what if the kid has all sorts of problems? What if he thinks it's okay to get into my stuff and he breaks my microscope or messes with Einstein? Maybe getting a baby wouldn't be so bad after all.

CHAPTER 10

The big state fair in Puyallup happens at the end of September, and we go every year. This year, Master Rickman had selected Khal and me, along with some others, to represent our *dojang* on one of the stages.

Dad pulled our car into the dusty parking lot. Gladys kept pointing and shouting, "There's a space!" which I could see in the rearview mirror was really getting under Dad's skin.

"I can see the spaces, Mama. The parking lot's practically empty." The gates hadn't been open that long.

"Then why have you passed up a dozen perfectly fine ones?" Gladys patted the large, multicolored straw purse she always brought to the fair. For now, the bag was empty. "I want to get inside and get me some freebies."

Dad parked. My stiff white *do bok* crinkled as I

climbed out. The uniform was brand-new—from my parents for my birthday. I walked around to the other side to help Gladys out, even though she always shoos me away when I do that.

"Just take his arm, Mama."

"I'm a senior, not a corpse. The only time I plan to need help getting in or out of someplace is the day you put me in the ground."

"So you'll climb into your own coffin?" Dad smirked.

Mom spoke smoothly from outside the passenger door. "Miss Gladys, I know you want your grandson to be a gentleman."

"Yeah, Gladys. Give me a chance to show you Tae Kwon Do's first tenet." Gladys knows the five tenets as well as I do. She likes to remind me of them now and then. Tenet number one is courtesy.

Gladys scowled. "Oh, all right." She gripped my forearm and stepped out onto the packed dirt ground. "I suppose it's good for you to get some practice, since any day now you'll be bringing home the girls."

"What? No, I won't!" Jeez. First Grandpa Ed and now Gladys. Why was everyone obsessed with girlfriends all of a sudden?

Gladys patted my cheek. "My milk chocolate's so handsome. And getting so tall!" She raised one eyebrow. "But don't forget, it's your mom you passed up. I've still got a half inch on you."

I had a feeling I'd be hearing that a lot, at least until I outgrew her, too. "Not for long, you won't." I gave her a smile and we walked toward the entrance.

Only ten feet inside the fairgrounds, Gladys stopped at a booth selling spa tubs with whirlpool jets. "Mama, what are you doing?" Dad asked. "You're not going to buy one of those things."

"You know that and I know that." Gladys held up her straw bag. "But I smell a freebie."

We kept walking while Gladys pretended to be interested in Jacuzzis.

A few minutes later, Gladys strode toward us with a new plastic visor on her head. "How's this for a first score?" She tipped her head so we could read the print on the visor: BENNY'S SPAS AND JETS. "No sun in my eyes today, thank you very much!"

"Great, Mama. Let's go." Dad turned and kept walking.

"You're not impressed now, but just wait. In a few hours, when you've got yourself a tension headache from squinting, you'll be wishing you had one."

Dad pulled out his cop sunglasses and put them on. "I'm good."

We continued down the wide paved road lined with vendor booths on either side and a row of food stands down the center. "Breakfast time!" Gladys shouted. She made a beeline for the little house on wheels that sold Cow Chip Cookies—"a fair favorite since 1935"—and

Alienade, a radioactive-yellow drink that looked like Gladys's favorite pop, Mountain Dew.

I didn't even bother asking if I could have what Gladys was having since Mom believes eating a healthy breakfast is the key to world peace. She'd given me Raisin Bran, peanut butter toast, and a giant fruit-and-yogurt smoothie before we'd left. I would wait until after our Tae Kwon Do demo, and then I'd pig out.

After Gladys got her cookie and drink, we went to find Grandpa Ed. The rock club always has a display in the hobbies area, although I hadn't known that until recently. Even though we go to the fair every year, I'd never gone into Hobby Hall. I'd figured it was all quilts and dolls and that needlepoint stuff. And of course Mom had never mentioned Grandpa Ed being there, since, until this past summer, she hadn't talked to him for ten years.

"Here it is," I said, pointing to the sign hanging from the building.

Glass showcases full of people's crafts filled the rooms. What I noticed most of all were the ribbons. I imagined one of the big blue ones hanging in my room. NATIONAL SCIENCE COMPETITION — FIRST PLACE, it would say.

We walked through a room full of collections. I couldn't believe some of the stuff people collected: cookie jars, lunch boxes, Pez dispensers, Holstein-patterned everything.

Finally, we came to the room where a large PUYALLUP ROCK CLUB banner hung on the wall behind a table. Morgan and her dad were there, talking to what looked like a mom and dad and their two kids. One of the kids had just spun a roulette wheel and Morgan was giving him a mineral sample for a prize.

Grandpa Ed stood to the side, speaking with another lady. Behind him, a large display case protected the model of the Space Needle he'd shown me at the September rock club meeting. He and a buddy had made it themselves, all out of petrified wood! It was impressive—almost as tall as I was. Grandpa Ed had said he'd help me make something, if I wanted. He'd suggested a car, but I was thinking a petrified-wood microscope would look ultracool in my room.

When Morgan saw us, her smile grew to half the size of her face. She bounced over. "Hi, Brendan!" I barely had time to say hi before she was introducing herself to my family. "Hi! Are you Brendan's mom and dad? I'm Morgan. Brendan and I go to school together. We're science partners. Brendan probably told you."

I hadn't.

"It's nice to meet you, Morgan," Mom said, shaking her hand.

Morgan reached for Dad's hand, as well. "Hello," Dad said.

"Ah-*hmm*." Gladys cleared her throat. She eyed me.

The expression on her face looked a little too much like gloating. "What was that I was saying in the parking lot?"

Gladys's question was like a poke in my rear. I jumped in before she could open her big mouth again. "This is my grandma. You probably won't see her around much."

Morgan gave me a funny look, but just as quick her smile was back. "It's an honor to meet you, Mrs. Buckley."

"Oh, no, child. Just Gladys will do."

Finally, Grandpa Ed walked up.

"Are you ready to go?" I asked.

"Yessirree! To the cow barn! Morgan, you coming?"

She looked excited. "I'd—"

"We don't really need help," I jumped in again.

"Help with what?" Mom asked.

I glanced at Grandpa Ed. "Uh . . . just something we need for our science project."

Dad's forehead wrinkled. "In the cow barn?"

"Yeah. Remember that competition I told you about?"

Dad nodded, but he still looked skeptical.

"For our experiment, we need some . . . manure."

"*Manure?*" Dad said loudly. The family that had been at the rock club table and now stood around the petrified Space Needle glanced our way.

"How exactly will you be getting that manure home?" Gladys asked, looking me up and down. "Surely not in the same car with *me*."

Morgan jumped in then. "We don't need that much, Mrs.—I mean, Gladys."

"Yeah," I said, glad that I wasn't fighting this one on my own. "Just a medium-sized Tupperware container."

"Tupperware container?" Mom's eyes got wide. "Brendan, you could have at least asked."

"Sorry. Can I use one of your Tupperware containers?" Of course, I already had it in my duffel bag.

"What exactly are you planning to do with this cow manure?" Dad asked.

"Well," Morgan said. I'd let her take this one. "We're going to mix it with other forms of biomass with the hypothesized result of increasing its overall energy output."

When Morgan and I had gotten together to decide on our project, we'd concluded—with Mr. H's encouragement—that my original idea of experimenting on human poop might be too unhygienic for a school-related competition, not to mention it would be a hard sell with our parents.

Dad stared at me, his eyebrows as flat as a corpse's EKG. "Couldn't you build a rocket or something?"

Cow poop obviously wasn't going over much better.

Grandpa Ed spoke. "It may not be glamorous, but these kids' subject matter is on the cutting edge of fuel technology."

Dad's eyebrow EKG showed signs of life. "You're telling me cow dung is on the cutting edge of something?" He turned to me. "Brendan, does your subject matter really have to be *fecal* matter?"

"I was planning to tell you my idea, but you've been so busy. . . ."

"You should be proud of the boy. He's got a sharp mind and he wants to use it for good." My shoulder tingled where Grandpa Ed's hand rested.

Dad's jaw clenched. "You don't need to tell me about my own son." He looked at me. "You're wearing your new *do bok*. I think it can wait until after your demonstration."

I tugged at my clean uniform. "I'll be careful."

"I checked with a buddy of mine over there," Grandpa Ed said. "They're taking the cows out this morning to sanitize the place. We wait too long and there won't be a speck of the stuff anywhere."

"If that's the case, I'm sure there'll be a Dumpster full of it *somewhere*," Dad said.

"We need it to be as fresh as possible," I said.

"What? Straight from the cow's patootie?" Gladys's lips stretched in disgust.

Mom spoke finally. "Let's just go get it. The kids need it for their project."

Yes! I could always count on Mom to support my scientific pursuits. I said goodbye to Morgan, who frowned a little but got excited again when she saw a girl standing at the rock club table. "Bye! I'll see you at the Tae Kwon Do demonstration if I can get away."

You don't have to, I thought, but I just waved, then hurried after Mom. Dad followed last. Outside the building, I turned right. "I think the cows are this way."

"Yes, they are," Gladys said. "Next to Lulu's Dairy Barn. From cow to cone. Can't get any fresher than that!" She hoisted her straw purse over her shoulder. Already, the freebies bag was bulging with stuff.

I led the way to the red buildings in the distance. The cattle pens have never been my favorite place to visit at the fair. First of all, they stink. Second of all, they stink. No offense to anyone who raises cows or sees them as sacred or collects cows and cow-related paraphernalia, but they *stink*.

So I wasn't exactly looking forward to the task ahead, but then, after reading up on cow dung's hidden potential, I had to admit I had a new respect for the animal.

We approached the Pig Palace, a small covered area adjacent to the cow barns. A person in a big pink pig costume stood in front, waving. "There he is!" Gladys hollered. "My hunka hunka piece of pork!" The rest of us looked at each other like, *Do you know this lady?*

"Kate, come take my picture." Gladys always makes sure to get a picture with the Puyallup Pig. "After that, we can watch Big Mama feed all her little pig babies. Unlike Brendan, I won't be needing any freebies from the cattle pens."

Gladys handed Mom her camera and hurried to stand next to Porky. Dad followed Grandpa Ed and me into the thick stench. I coughed a couple of times. Maybe I *was* crazy to want to do an experiment with this stuff. No, it was only a small amount. I could handle it.

The barn was crammed full of cows—brown, black, white with black splotches, babies, mamas, and bulls. They stood in their gated pens on either side of a hard-packed dirt aisle. Hanging overhead were those red, white, and blue semicircular banners like you might see on a big old house in the South.

A bull with pointy horns eyed me suspiciously. He stamped his hooves and blew nasty breath from his nose. His tail twitched back and forth. I wouldn't be getting anywhere near *that* rear end. People were leading cows out of their stalls already. We'd have to work quickly.

I looked into the nearest pen. *Dang.* All the manure was coated in sawdust. That would affect the results of our experiment for sure. Although wood *was* biomass . . . maybe we could factor that in somehow. Or maybe I really *should* try to get the droppings straight from the source, as Gladys had suggested.

The air filled with the sound of tiny squeals. Cows mooed and moved about nervously. Something squawked. I looked around. Where was all that noise coming from?

A stampede! At least a dozen small pigs rushed toward us down the center aisle. Behind the piglets ran a teenager, clutching a bag. A bulging, multicolored straw bag.

Gladys appeared in the barn, huffing and puffing. "Stop that hoodlum!" She shook her fist in the air. "Thief! Thief!"

I stepped into the boy's path with my arms extended. He shoved me out of the way, turned at the end of the row of stalls, and headed into the next barn.

I regained my balance, dropped my bag, and ran.

The boy exited the barn, headed toward the Slush Factory ("Twenty-eight flavors to mix!") and Dumbo's Jumbos Elephant Ears.

I turned on my turbojets and sprinted even faster. I glanced over my shoulder at the sound of someone running behind me. Dad.

Suddenly, both my feet were up in the air. I hung suspended for what seemed like forever, waiting for my body to hit the packed dirt. Instead, the ground squished. A funky smell filled my nostrils. I laid my head on the ground and moaned. The fresh cow pie under my hip was still warm from the oven.

Dad sprinted past.

"You all right, there?" Grandpa Ed pulled me to my feet.

I nodded. My butt hurt, and I was hot from embarrassment, but other than that I was fine. My *do bok,* on the other hand . . . I twisted my head, trying to get a look at the damage.

"That's quite a tire tread you got there."

I groaned. "Dad's going to kill me."

"Excuse me." A woman with a shovel moved in. "We need to get this up before anyone else steps in it. Or what's left of it, anyways." She glanced at my behind. "There's a men's restroom right over there." She pointed past a Dumpster labeled DOO-DOO ONLY.

"Can you wait just a second?" I asked the lady. "I can help you with that." Grandpa Ed had picked up my duffel bag. I zipped it open and pulled out Mom's Tupperware container and gardening spade.

"It's certainly fresh," Grandpa Ed said. "I think I see some steam coming off it."

I scooped up a shovelful, plopped it into the container, and snapped on the lid. The woman looked at me like I was nuts. "I'm not even going to ask," she said. "All done?"

"Yes, ma'am. Thank you." I wrapped the little shovel in the old towel I'd brought and dropped everything back into the bag.

"We'd better get you cleaned up," Grandpa Ed said. We walked toward the bathroom. When we passed the area behind Dumbo's Jumbos, two uniformed security officers held the boy by his arms. Dad was there, too, holding Gladys's straw bag. He glanced our way. I hurried into the bathroom.

After I'd used up almost a whole roll of wet paper towels on my *do bok*, and then taken care of some of my own business, we came out. On my backside was a large light brown stain shaped like Australia. The rest of my family waited near the restroom exit. Gladys had her bag securely over her arm. She munched on a Krusty Pup corn dog.

"Are you all right?" Mom asked. "Gladys said you fell pretty hard."

"Not before he diverted the juvenile delinquent right into the hands of the authorities. Opening the pigpen for kicks, then running off with my bag." Gladys scowled. "What's wrong with people?"

"Well, all's well that ends well, I guess," Mom said. "Did you get what you came for?"

"Mission accomplished." I grinned, then got serious when I saw Dad's face. He eyed the stain. His mouth pulled to one side.

Gladys linked her free arm with mine. "You're my hero, Milk Chocolate!" She got a glimmer in her eye. "Speaking of chocolate, let's go get some of that delicious ice cream from Lulu's."

"You're going to be sorry, Mama," Dad said. "The way you're eating."

Gladys patted her bag. "Thanks to my grandson, I've still got my Rolaids. Pop a few of those pep pills, and I'll be good to go." Gladys's nose wrinkled as she unlinked her arm. "I love you, kid, but for now, I think I'll keep my distance."

"We need to go," Dad said. "Master Rickman was expecting Brendan five minutes ago."

When we arrived at the stage, Morgan came up behind me. "Hi, Brendan!"

I turned quickly, feeling suddenly very warm in my poop-stained uniform.

"Did you get the manure?"

"Yeah, no problem." I tugged on my damp, smelly *do bok* and glanced around. Did she have to talk so loud?

"I wish my mom were here to see you perform," Morgan said. "She's out on the research vessel this weekend."

"That's all right," I said, relieved that she *wasn't* there. "It's not that big of a deal."

Dad called my name.

"I've got to go. See you later." I walked backward until Morgan finally turned away. When I looked again, she was sitting next to Mom. *Great.*

I found Khal behind the platform and started to warm up with the other students, though I was still plenty warm from the encounter with Morgan.

"What's on your uniform?" Khal asked. "Someone spill their coffee?"

"You don't want to know." Truth was, I didn't want him to know. I'd never hear the end of it.

"Wait a minute. That's not . . ."

"I said you don't want to know."

"Aw, man! You're not standing next to *me* out there! I don't want to smell that mess. And no way am I sitting next to you on Extreme Scream." Extreme Scream is a ride that lifts you a few hundred feet up a tower, then drops you in about two seconds. Khal and I *always* ride Extreme Scream together.

"You can't even smell it," I said. "I washed it off."

Khal's eyes slid in the direction of the audience. "I bet the Belcher will ride it with you." He grabbed me around the shoulders and pretended to be scared. "Oooh," he made his voice go high, "Brendan! Save me! Save me! Ew, what's that horrible *smell*? Oh, it's probably just me. Oooh! Brendan, Brendan! You're so *beautiful*!"

I shoved him away. "Knock it off."

Dad eyed us from the front row.

"Fine," I said. "Don't stand next to me. I don't care." Actually, I did, but I was mad at Khal for making fun of me. And mad at myself for doing a back flop onto a cow pie. Now I had to perform in front of a big crowd—a crowd that included Morgan, which didn't really matter, but still, she *was* a girl from school—with a huge poop stain on my butt!

I punched, kicked, jumped, and blocked, trying to keep my body to the front as much as possible. If I had to spin, I did it as fast as I could. I saw a lady whisper and point. She was probably saying to the person next to her, *What's that big blotch on that boy's jacket? It looks like Australia!*

Finally, we were bowing to Master Rickman and everyone was applauding. The crowd started to disperse.

Morgan ran up as soon as I got off the stage and gushed like a geyser about what a great job I'd done. Khal fluttered his eyelids behind her back. I ignored him.

"Go change your clothes," Dad said. "I hope you know how to work with bleach."

"Yes, sir," I said. I found the nearest bathroom and took my time changing.

Fortunately, when I came out, Morgan had taken off with her dad to check out the rest of the fair. Khal and I headed for Extreme Scream. We rode it five times in a row—until my head felt like it was still stuck somewhere up in the clouds and my stomach couldn't take one more drop. Then we headed to the nearest snack booth and loaded up on Cow Chip Cookies.

CHAPTER 11

"She's such an expressive, articulate girl," Mom said as we sat at the table finishing our lunch the next day. Dad was at the library studying. This wasn't the first time Mom had said something about Morgan since meeting her at the fair.

"Yeah, she's loud and talkative, all right," I said.

Mom's lips pulled down as if she disapproved, but I could tell she was only half serious. "Are you excited about setting up your experiment?"

Morgan would be arriving soon with the things she'd agreed to bring: a scale, disposable gloves like they wear in doctors' offices, and sixteen round latex balloons. She also said she could contribute at least eight two-liters. We needed sixteen of them, as well—fifteen for holding the manure mixtures, and one that we'd leave empty as a control.

"I guess."

"That sounded less than enthusiastic."

"It's just . . . I like to work on my own."

"Hmmm." Mom bit into her sandwich.

The doorbell rang.

"Well, I'm sure you'll make a great team," Mom said. "Let me know if you need anything."

Yeah, like being saved from getting talked to death, I thought. I took my dishes to the kitchen and headed down the stairs. It had been my idea to keep the experiment at my house. I wanted to be the one to do the twice-daily measurements. Fortunately, Morgan hadn't fought me about it. "It was mainly your idea, after all," she'd said. Plus, she had pets that roamed freely at her house, whereas mine was confined to his tank.

As I turned the doorknob, my stomach squeezed. Was I nervous? No way. Why would I be nervous?

Morgan held up two plastic bags of two-liters. "Washed and ready to go." She stepped inside. "And here's the other stuff." She handed me another bag.

Why was she staring at my mouth?

"Were you eating lunch?" she asked.

"Yeah, but we're done."

She pointed at my face. I pulled back. "You've got some peanut butter—"

I swiped at my lips and wiped the sticky stuff on my sweats.

"I like crunchy, too." Morgan flashed her glittery smile.

"I—I mean, we—we should get started." I turned quickly and headed toward the basement.

"Oh, can I *please* meet Einstein first?"

I stopped halfway down the stairs. We had a lot of work to do and not much time to do it, but I kind of liked the idea of showing off my lizard. "All right." I came back to the landing. "He's in my room."

Morgan grinned.

"We can leave the bags here." We leaned over at the same time to set our bags down, and I caught a whiff of her hair. It smelled kind of good. Like green apple Jolly Ranchers. Not that I cared. It was just an observation.

We headed upstairs.

"Hi, Morgan." Mom poked her head out from the kitchen.

"Hi, Mrs. Buckley. Brendan's introducing me to Einstein."

Mom smiled. "Great."

I kept walking before they could start up a conversation. We had work to do. Plus, the last thing I needed was a girl from school getting too friendly with my mom.

We went down the hall to my bedroom. Einstein was on his rock, taking in the heat. Morgan moved slowly and whispered as if she knew he might flee at any loud sounds. "Ohhh, what a cute little guy! May I hold him?"

She wanted to *hold* him? "Anoles don't like to be

handled too much." I didn't want her to know that I hadn't yet held my own lizard, mostly because the guy at the pet store had said that for little guys, they can bite pretty good. As a scientist, I usually like to observe things directly, but that wasn't something I felt the need to experience firsthand.

"Who told you that?"

"The guy at the pet store." I crossed my arms. "And the reptile vet." Was she going to start being a know-it-all again? If only I could do this experiment on my own. "Besides, we don't have time." I glanced at my watch with the built-in altimeter. My room was still 119 feet above sea level, but it was no longer one o'clock—the time we were supposed to get started. It was 1:17 already.

"If you're worried about him getting away . . ."

I was, actually. The pet store guy had said anoles are master escape artists.

"He won't. I know exactly what to do. Dad and I caught anoles all the time in Florida."

"You caught them?"

"Yeah. In our backyard."

"In your *yard*?" I felt my eyebrows pop up.

"Of course. They were all over the place. We even had one living in our house for a while—Twiggy. Dad and I loved to observe his behavior. Once Twiggy was used to us, we held him all the time."

"Wow." I couldn't imagine doing something like that with my dad. He isn't exactly an Animal Planet kind of guy. And he still wasn't crazy about me having Einstein. Just the other night he'd asked if I was sure I didn't want a dog instead.

"So, can I? It'll make me feel like I'm back home." Morgan's brown eyes gazed at me hopefully. I'd never thought about the fact that she might miss living in Florida.

I glanced at the tank. If she really was as experienced as she said she was, maybe this was my chance to learn how to pick up Einstein and hold him, too. I'd been putting off changing the substrate in his tank because I wasn't sure how to capture him and put him in the small cage we'd gotten for that purpose.

I closed my bedroom door. "Okay."

She clasped her hands together. "Awesome!" She started to take off the tank's lid.

"I'll do it," I said, annoyed. Maybe she had more experience with anoles than me, but this was still *my* anole. And *my* terrarium. I slid the lid just enough so that Morgan could get her hand into the tank. I spoke calmly and quietly. "It's okay, Einstein. Don't be afraid."

Einstein darted around behind the plastic hanging vines. Morgan held her hand steady. With one grab Einstein was in her cupped palms. It happened so quickly I didn't even get to see how she did it.

She kept him from wriggling away by keeping her thumb on the back of his neck. "I won't hurt you, little guy." She watched him intently. "Sometimes they poop on you in self-defense, but it's so tiny it's no big deal."

My eyes widened. She liked the idea of experimenting on cow manure, she wanted to hold my lizard, *and* she didn't mind getting pooped on? Morgan was unlike any girl *I'd* ever met. She held up Einstein and let his long nose tickle the bottom of her ear.

"What are you doing?" My voice rose in concern. I reached out to protect my lizard just as he opened his mouth and chomped down on her earlobe.

A shout jumped out of my mouth before I could stop it.

Morgan let go.

Einstein dangled from her ear like an earring!

"My friend Beth and I used to do this all the time. It doesn't hurt, if that's what you're worried about."

I wasn't. I was worried about my pet.

"Their teeth are so small it just feels like someone pinching you with their fingernails."

"Take him off!" I didn't want to frighten Einstein, but I couldn't keep my voice calm and quiet this time. "Take him *off*." I sure hoped he'd poop on her now. It would serve her right. "He's turning brown!"

She grasped his thin body and he let go.

"Put him back," I said firmly.

Morgan set Einstein in the tank and he scrambled under his tree bark. "It doesn't hurt them," she said.

My hands shook as I secured the tank. A lizard hanging from an earlobe just wasn't right. The sight had made me woozy. Not that I would ever admit to that. "He's not a piece of jewelry." I knew I sounded mad, but I didn't care.

I blew out my breath, trying to regain my *guk gi*—self-control. Einstein would be all right, but this girl was crazier than I'd thought. My doubts about working with her boiled and bubbled like the baking soda–vinegar experiment I'd tried once. "Let's go," I said. If we were going to win this contest, I would have to take charge.

We collected the things we'd left near the front door, then continued on to the basement and into the garage, where I'd already gathered everything else we needed: more two-liters; duct tape; small, precut squares of waxed paper; a funnel; distilled water; mashed bananas; vegetable peels from last night's stir-fry; and of course, the manure.

Morgan set up the scale on Dad's workbench, which I'd covered with a plastic tarp in case anything spilled. If we left even a trace of cow in this garage, Dad would *have* a cow.

Morgan and I had decided to do three tests, and five trials of each test. Five bottles would hold only manure—another control test; five bottles would hold cow manure plus mashed banana; five bottles would hold cow manure plus vegetable peelings; and one bottle would be empty to show whether there was any change in the volume of the air due to differences in temperature or barometric pressure from beginning to end. Sixteen bottles. We labeled the two-liters with a permanent marker on masking tape. So far, so good.

Next, we put on our gloves. "I'll measure," I said. "You can put the biomass in the bottles."

"Can I measure? I'm very exact."

"So am I." I crossed my arms.

"I'm kind of clumsy when it comes to pouring. I'm always spilling stuff."

I *had* seen her wiping up her drink at lunch more than once. "All right."

Morgan put a square of waxed paper on the scale. She scooped some of the cow manure with a plastic spoon and put it on the paper. She could have been scooping ice cream, the way she was grinning.

I dropped my arms and moved in to watch. The smell wasn't as bad as being in the cow barn, but it was still pretty gross. I breathed through my mouth.

After she'd finished measuring three samples, she handed me the spoon. "I guess we could both take a turn."

I smiled. "Thanks." I didn't care what Khalfani thought. Measuring poop was fun.

After I had carefully weighed a few, I handed the spoon back to Morgan. Without needing to say much at all, we fell into an assembly-line rhythm: me handing Morgan a waxed paper square, her weighing the sample, me taking it and poking it into a two-liter. I held the funnel while she poured the filtered water, we both screwed on lids and gave each bottle a good shake; then she held the bottles while I taped the balloons to their mouths. We worked together like the gears on a well-oiled bike. I had to admit, we were a pretty good team.

We had worked quickly, not wanting to let the first bottles we finished have too much of a head start on the others, which could affect our results. Morgan had stayed quiet the whole time, completely focused on the job. I was surprised—and impressed.

When we were done, we washed our hands in the downstairs bathroom, then carefully carried the bottles into our basement rec room, where I usually practiced Tae Kwon Do and Khal and I sometimes sparred. We lined up the bottles against the back wall and along one side, as well—they took up more space than I expected—and I opened the small window for ventilation. Mr. H had strongly warned us that our bottles needed to be placed in a well-ventilated area and couldn't be anywhere near an open flame or sparks of electricity, since—assuming everything went as it should in the anaerobic conditions inside the bottles—bacteria in the poop would soon start producing methane, a highly flammable gas. The gas would inflate the balloons, and I'd measure their circumference twice a day to compare production.

The most important variable for us to control was

room temperature. Mr. H had said we'd have the best luck at methane creation if we kept the temperature as close to thirty-five degrees Celsius as possible. Even though Dad wasn't too happy about it at first because of how it would impact our electricity bill, he eventually agreed to let me keep a portable heater on in the room over the course of our experiment. I was glad he didn't ask how hot thirty-five degrees Celsius is. I didn't want to have to tell him our basement was going to feel like summertime in Tucson, Arizona, for the next two weeks.

We made sure the humming heater was as equidistant from the bottles as possible, checked and recorded the barometric pressure using the barometer Grandpa Ed had loaned me, and went back to the garage to clean up.

I didn't look at my watch again until Morgan was climbing into her dad's car in our driveway: 4:28.

The three hours had flown by.

CHAPTER 12

"The ones with bananas are going gangbusters!" I told Morgan as we put our stuff in our lockers before school. I didn't really like for the guys to see me with her, but over the past three days, walking to homeroom had become our time to check in about the experiment's progress.

"Interesting." Morgan's eyes narrowed and her lips pooched. "I wonder if it could have anything to do with the bananas' high sugar content."

I nodded. It was a solid hypothesis. We closed our lockers and started walking.

"Thanks for keeping the bottles at your house and for doing all the measuring. Our cat, Tee, is supercurious, and Rex, our retriever, is ultrahyper. They'd have knocked the bottles over and popped the balloons by now."

"Tee and Rex. That's funny."

"My dad's idea. A little paleontology humor."

Wow. To have parents who made science jokes. *That would be so cool.*

Right before we reached homeroom, Dwight David ran up. He wore his fatigues again, which he did at least a couple of times a week. "Hi, Morgan!" he said, grinning up at her. He was probably four inches shorter than she was.

He ignored me, but I didn't care. A small, round white scar on his cheek stood out against his brown skin. Khal said Dwight David had gotten the scar from a BB gun battle, which had impressed Khal but sounded crazy to me.

"Hi, Dwight David. How are you?" Morgan sounded as if she was genuinely interested.

Dwight David held out a gigantic bag of M&Ms. "I hope you like them."

Morgan looked a little surprised, but she took the bag in her hands. "I *love* M&Ms."

Dwight David grinned. "That's good, because they're for you."

"You brought all these for *me?*"

Cordé walked by just then. "Oooh, look at little Romeo! Giving his girlfriend a big bag of candy!"

Dwight David shoved Cordé, who continued toward homeroom, pointing out Dwight David's gift to a handful of other guys along the way.

"Gosh. A whole pound of M&Ms." Morgan looked flushed. "Um, thanks, Dwight David."

I had started to mind being ignored. "The bell's about to ring," I said.

Morgan unzipped her backpack and put the candy inside. "I'll share some with you later," she said as we moved toward the door.

I started to say thanks, but she wasn't looking at me. She was looking at Dwight David. I hitched my backpack higher and followed them into the room. So what if Dwight David had given her a pound of M&Ms? What did I care?

If Morgan was really smart, though, she'd watch out for that kid. Dwight David was like a loaded spring, constantly getting tripped. It was only the beginning of October and he'd already spent more time in the vice principal's office than all the rest of the kids in the sixth grade combined, usually for something he'd done in our World Civilizations class. He and Mrs. Simmons were turning out to be like methane and a spark—a volatile combination.

The last time I'd seen Dwight David get kicked out of class, it was because he'd stood up and yelled "Yes, ma'am!" at the top of his lungs whenever Mrs. Simmons said "Is that clear, class?"—which she did about a hundred times each day. It only took three times of Dwight David shouting—after she'd warned him twice to stop—for him to get sent to Vice Principal Bowman.

Morgan took her assigned seat, which was next to mine since Ms. Manley did her seating chart alphabetically. When Ms. Manley got up to close the door, Dwight David whispered, "Psst, Morgan."

Morgan peered around me. I was curious what else Dwight David had to say to her, but I resisted the temptation to look. Until Morgan sucked in her breath.

Dwight David's eyebrows undulated up and down—one and then the other in smooth succession. He was doing the wave with his eyebrows! Usually I didn't think Dwight David's shenanigans, as Gladys would call them, were very funny, but this was actually really cool.

Ms. Manley turned before Dwight David expected. Everyone who had been oohing and aahing got quiet real quick.

We all waited to see what would happen to Dwight David *this* time.

"Well, Mr. Del Santos," Ms. Manley said, "that *is* entertaining. But tell me, can you do this?" Without warning, Ms. Manley's eyeballs started to go around and around in tiny circles, gyrating like a compass next to a magnet. The whole class gasped at once. No one could believe it!

After that, Dwight David hung on Ms. Manley's every word—we *all* did—as if she were the star of her own TV show or an NFL athlete, which, based on her musculature, she could have been.

Morgan and I spent lunch that day in Mr. Hammond's office talking about our experiment and Morgan's hypothesis about the bananas. He sipped his Coke and nodded a lot and told us to keep observing—we were on to something really good. After helping Mr. H finish off his Hershey bar, I started itching to get outside and throw the ball around with the guys. I thanked him, said goodbye to Morgan, and left to find Khal and the others.

"Where *you* been?" Khal threw the football to Marcus. "We need another player."

I almost said *Morgan and I*—but that would have been like handing myself over to a firing squad. "I was talking to Mr. Hammond about our experiment."

Khal rolled his eyes. "'*Our* experiment . . . *our* experiment.' Are you going to be talking about that every day for the next month?" He caught the ball back from Marcus.

"*No.* But we want to make it to the finalist round."

"Dwight and I are going to make a wicked cool launcher." Khal threw the ball to Oscar, who fumbled it and dropped it on the ground.

"Dwight *David*," Oscar corrected, bending over to pick up the ball. He lobbed it back to Khal. It wobbled in the air, but Khal still caught it.

"Dwight Dingleberry is more like it," Marcus said.

"I think he's hilarious. Anyway, this launcher's going to be like nothing you've ever seen. *Military* cool." Khal torpedoed the ball at me. I wasn't ready, and it bounced off my chest and onto the grass. "So, don't you think you've been spending a little too much time with the Belcher?"

Ever since the first day of school, most of the boys in our homeroom called Morgan that, and not only behind her back. Most of them, including Khal, let out loud, long burps whenever she walked by. I would never do that, but I wasn't about to tell them to stop, either.

"Only as much as I have to for our—the experiment," I said, picking up the ball and shooting it back.

"Yeah, well, seems to me like maybe you *like* her or something." Khal made it sound as if liking Morgan would be a federal offense. He threw the ball again, hard. It stung my hands.

"I don't! Now can we just play ball?" I hurled the football once more.

Khal ducked, narrowly escaping getting his bell rung. "Hey! Watch it!"

I hadn't meant for the pass to be so high. I'm just taller than Khal. But I guess I hadn't exactly been aiming for his hands, either.

Khal muttered something about me being too serious; then he motioned for Oscar to go long and launched the ball overhead. Oscar took off running, but when he reached for the ball, he stumbled and face-planted. The ball hit the ground a few feet past where he lay and bounced away. He sat up slowly, rubbed his head, and looked around.

"I guess we'll find out Friday night," Khal said.

"Find out what?" I asked.

"You're going to the dance, aren't you?"

"Yeah, I guess." I hadn't been sure if I would, but Mom, who was on the PTA board this year, had signed herself up as a chaperone, so it was kind of just assumed I'd be there, and since I didn't really care one way or the other, I went along with it. Fortunately, Dad had to work on a paper for school and couldn't be recruited. One parent as a chaperone was all right. Two was not. Knowing Dad, he would have come in his uniform.

"So, I guess we'll find out how you really feel about the Belcher on Friday night—when she asks you to dance." Khal grinned.

My stomach dropped. Somehow I needed to contract a terribly contagious disease in the next forty-eight hours.

I was a scientist. Surely I could come up with something.

Log Entry—Thursday, October 4

Only twenty-four hours until the dance and I'm showing no symptoms of anything other than puberty. No hives, no rashes, no oozing, pus-filled sores. Unless you count the four pimples that suddenly appeared on my forehead this morning.

Aghhh! What am I going to do if she asks me to dance?

CHAPTER 13

Friday night rolled around, and boy, was I in trouble. As much as I wanted to be sick in bed—too hoarse to speak, too weak to dance, and most importantly, too contagious to go anywhere—I was fine. Except for my stomach, which felt like an empty cement mixer on overdrive.

I had spent the afternoon cleaning out Einstein's tank. I'd lured him into his holding pen with a mealworm. Even though I'd been nervous he'd try to make a break for it, he ran right in. Easy. Cleaning the tank, on the other hand, was *hard*. It took me a good couple of hours to get everything out, wash the walls, replace the bark, and put everything back in. I was glad when it was over.

I took a quick shower and threw on some clothes—a red, green, and black plaid shirt with snaps down the front, my faded black jeans, and my red-checkered slip-on Vans. Not that I cared what I looked like so much, but if I was going to go to the dance, I might as well show up looking halfway decent.

I crouched and peered into Einstein's tank. Einstein stared at me from his rock. "What do you think, Einstein? Should I dance with her?" His snout moved from side to side, as if he were shaking his head no. "Totally! But what if she comes right out and asks me?" It seemed like something she would do. "I can't just say no."

Einstein clambered onto the vine and disappeared into the ivy. "Yeah, my thought exactly. Make up an excuse, then run for cover." I pulled out the sprayer and misted the leaves. "Well, wish me luck, buddy. I'll let you know how it goes."

On my way down the hall, I stepped into the bathroom and put on one more dose of deodorant. If I actually ended up dancing, I didn't want to be stinking the place up.

"Have a great time, buddy," Dad said as I walked into the kitchen. "Dance one for me."

Mom put her hands on Dad's chest and gazed into his eyes. "Remember the first time we danced?"

Dad pecked her on the lips. "How could I forget?" He spun her around the kitchen, then wrapped his arms around her waist. They swayed in the middle of the "dance floor." I was thinking about heading back to my room. The mush factor was getting a little too high for me.

"That was the night I knew we were meant to be together," Mom said.

One dance with someone could tell you something like *that*? I was skeptical, but a little curious. What *would* I do if Morgan asked me to dance? All the guys would be right there, watching. Just the thought of it made me feel like I might hyperventilate.

"We ought to get going," Mom said, giving Dad another peck. She rubbed her hand on my back. "You look very handsome, honey."

"Thanks," I said. Did the girls at my school think I was handsome? Did I want them to?

"Looking fly *is* tactical step number one," Dad said, "but if you *really* want to attract the honeybees . . ."

My ears warmed with embarrassment, but they were also tuned in to hear what Dad had to say.

He leaned in. "It's all about the scent. You want to borrow some of my cologne?" Mom stood with her arms folded, a half smile on her face. I kept expecting her to say something about me being too young, but she didn't.

"What do you say? I'll go get it for you." Dad started toward the door.

I swallowed. I'd been stung by a bee once. It hurt—bad. "Uh, that's okay. Thanks anyway."

If only I had come down with the measles.

Inside Eastmont's main entrance, a large poster board stood on an easel, directing kids to different rooms for different activities. The gym was open for shooting hoops, and hair and nails were being done in Room 3A. The cafeteria was where the actual dancing was going on. I could hear music. Lots of kids were already there, heading in groups from the gym to the cafeteria or the other way around. Some hung around in the entryway.

"Hey, Brendan!" Oscar came toward us. His dark hair was spiked up with gel and it was—*blue!*

"I'll see you in there, Bren," Mom whispered. "I've got to check in with the PTA people."

I nodded and she walked away. Oscar rushed up. "What do you think? Pretty cool, huh?" His eyeballs rolled side to side as if he were trying to see his own hair. He wore a dress shirt and tie, which were actually clean and not too wrinkled.

"Uh, yeah. Did you do it yourself?"

"No, a mom did it for me—in the hairstyling room. She spray-painted it!"

"You went in the hair and nails room? I thought it would be all girls in there."

"Exactly!" Oscar smiled big.

A couple of guys walked by with spray-painted hair—one red, the other blue-and-green-striped, same as the Seahawks' team colors. I hitched my thumb toward the cafeteria. "You want to go in?" My stomach had started to rumble. And the flyer for the dance had promised pizza.

The cafeteria was a lot brighter than I expected. The lights were on full force, I guessed so the adults could make sure no one was fooling around or doing something they shouldn't be doing.

Someone's older brother must have been recruited to be the DJ. He stood behind a table on the stage with his laptop open. Large speakers sat on either side of the table. Music played and kids were dancing. The only kids in the room who weren't dancing were scarfing down pizza at the food table. Khal and Marcus were among them.

Oscar and I headed over. Were those Lit'l Smokies on that platter?

"Hey, guys," I said, grabbing a toothpick and going straight for the little wieners. I chomped down on one. *Mmmm. Lit'l Smoky juice.*

"Os-car, my man, looking good!" Khal said. He bumped Oscar's fist. "I would have joined you, but I don't have much hair left to paint." He ran his hand over his newly shaved head. Whenever Khal got a haircut I kidded him about looking like a lightbulb.

I sniffed at the air around his scalp. "Are you wearing aftershave on your *head?*"

"Smells good, don't it?" He grinned.

Dwight David, looking like a regular kid in his polo

shirt and jeans instead of a military paratrooper, had come over to the table. He started downing one Lit'l Smoky after another.

Was the kid swallowing them whole? I had to get in there before they were all gone. We stabbed at the same time and came up with the same wiener. "You're hogging all the Lit'l Smokies," I said.

He smiled and shrugged. "They're good."

I couldn't disagree with that. I yanked my toothpick free and went for another one. As I bit down on the tiny sausage, Khal bumped me in the arm. "Look who's coming . . ."

I turned to see Morgan, in a *skirt*, headed straight for the food table, or to be more exact, headed straight for me!

I gulped down the rest of the Lit'l Smoky and hurried over to the big drink barrel at the end of the table. If she *was* coming after me, which from the look in her eyes she no doubt was, I didn't need the guys overhearing our whole conversation.

I grabbed a cup and started pouring orange drink from the big dispenser at the end of the table.

"Hi, Morgan!" I heard Dwight David say.

I looked. Dwight David had intercepted her. She glanced at me over the top of his head. I looked back down in time to see orange drink overflowing the edge of my cup.

"Dang," I said under my breath. I set the cup on the

table and hunted for some napkins to mop up the mess. When I stood again, Dwight David was leading Morgan by the hand to the middle of the dance floor. They disappeared into the mass of dancing kids.

Whew! I owed a big one to Dwight Dingleberry.

I looked around for my friends. Khal and Marcus had joined a circle of girls dancing on the fringes. Oscar had his hand in the bowl of Doritos. I headed toward him, but just as I got there, Shyla-Ann Thompson came up and asked if he wanted to dance. Oscar looked as if he'd just won the state lottery. "Sure!" He wiped his hands on his black pants, leaving a fluorescent streak of orange.

I gave Oscar a high five behind Shyla-Ann's back, and they headed off together.

I grabbed myself a piece of pepperoni pizza, then saw Mr. Hammond. I strode over to the wall where he leaned, bobbing his head to the music. "Hey, Mr. H!"

"Brendan! How's it going? You planning to"— Mr. Hammond's neck sort of snaked to one side and his shoulder jumped up to meet his ear—"bust a move?"

Was Mr. H trying to *pop*? "Careful, Mr. H, you might hurt yourself."

He laughed. I did, too. For the first time that night, I felt relaxed. I took another bite of pizza.

"Is there a special someone you've got your eye on?" He gestured with his head toward the dance floor.

"Me?" I pointed at my chest. "Nah. I'm too busy for girls. I'm trying to win a science contest!"

He nodded. "Of course. You can't afford any distractions right now."

"Exactly!" I stood with my back against the wall and finished off the slice. Mr. H understood what was important. I glanced toward the dance floor. Morgan bopped around in the middle of the crowd, smiling and laughing. Was she still dancing with Dwight David? He was so short it was hard to see him.

Whatever. What did I care who Morgan danced with? Or whether she was having a good time with Dwight David? They looked kind of ridiculous, really, the way she towered over him.

I turned to Mr. Hammond. "The banana-manure mixture seems to have peaked on its methane production," I said.

"That so?" Mr. H kept his eyes on the dance floor. His face broke into a big smile. "My wife just came in. I'll see you later, buddy." He took off across the cafeteria.

I was about to head back to the Lit'l Smokies when Lauren Dweck came up. Her lemon-yellow dress practically blinded me. Her hair was pinned up all over her head like a pile of curly fries.

"Hi, Brendan, do you want to dance?" She said it fast. I answered just as quickly, like a computer programmed for one response. "Okay." And like that, I was headed for the dance floor.

Another song had everyone bouncing, stepping, and jumping around. Oscar jiggled. Marcus jangled. Khal was popping—but for real, not like Mr. Hammond. Khal knew how to pop.

I started stepping side to side, mostly keeping my eyes on Khal, every once in a while smiling at Lauren so she wouldn't think I was ignoring her. I could see the back of Morgan's head. Her shiny brown hair reflected the lights above. She and Dwight David were still dancing, at the other end of the crowd that had flooded the floor with this latest song—the biggest hit of the night.

The next time I looked, Morgan was facing my direction. She looked at me just as Khal's hand snaked its way over to mine. Khal and I bumped fists.

Suddenly, I was in the flow, busting my robot moves. The current started in the fingers of the hand Khal had bumped then traveled along my arm, across my shoulders, and down my torso to my knees. When it reached my feet, I sent the current back up the other side and down my opposite arm. A few kids around me cheered and started to watch.

Khal and I had practiced these moves a lot at his house. We'd find guys popping on YouTube, then turn on music and try to imitate them. At home, I'd dance in front of my closet mirror to see what I looked like.

I kept the flow going, every once in a while throwing in a Tae Kwon Do move—a punch or a front kick. I was as smooth as creamy peanut butter.

The space around me had gotten bigger as kids stopped dancing to watch my moves. People clapped to the beat, including Mom, who I saw in the crowd. Cordé Wilkins pumped his fist in the air. Then the chant started: "Go Brendan! Go Brendan!"

A couple of girls stood in front, holding up their cell phones. Were they recording me with their video cameras? I flashed them a big smile.

I circled one last time around the empty space, pushing myself from toe to heel, heel to toe, sliding here and there as my knees bent and straightened, my hips wriggled, my torso went this way and that, and my arms undulated like the water in a wave machine. My head stayed steady and controlled at the top, like the knob on a joystick, telling the rest of my body what to do, which was to stay loose and fluid, until finally the song was over. I landed on one knee, and my chin dropped to my chest. Kids clapped and screamed. I looked up and grinned as the next tune came on.

I found Khal in the crowd and started to give him a high five, but he just scowled. "Jeez, man. You didn't have to steal the whole show."

Was Khal mad? He'd started the whole thing! And it wasn't like I *told* everyone to stop and watch.

I started to say sorry, but Lauren grabbed my hand and pulled me back into the crowd. "You were . . ." She gazed into my eyes, "*Awesome!*" She wrapped her arms around my neck, swaying to the music. I rocked stiffly, every once in a while glancing at Khal, who apparently had been grabbed by Melanie Sherman, because I didn't think Khal would ask someone the guys called Smellanie to dance, especially when his nose was only a little above her armpits. I sat next to Melanie in English. Her BO smelled like clam chowder.

The rest of the night was a blur. Every time I tried to leave the dance floor, another girl would ask me to dance, and every time, like that computer, I said okay. I guessed I was having fun after all. It seemed like the only girl I never danced with was Morgan. The problem I'd been so worried about ended up not being a problem at all.

Then why, I wondered as Mom and I left the dance, did I feel let down?

CHAPTER 14

Monday at my locker, I waited around for Morgan for our daily experiment update. The veggie-manure mix had edged out a couple of the manure-only bottles, and I wanted to get her take on it. When the five-minute bell rang and she still hadn't showed, I started toward homeroom.

A girl I sort of recognized, but not really, called out from a huddle in the hallway. "Hi, Brendan!"

I looked around. "Uh, hi," I said, and kept walking.

When I got to homeroom, it seemed like all the girls were staring at me. Lauren and Julia looked at each other and giggled.

The one girl who wasn't there was Morgan. Where was she? I had important developments to report. We were on day nine of our fourteen-day experiment. On the home stretch.

Khalfani only barely said hi. He was busy razzing Dwight David. "You better watch out, Dwight David. You spent a whole lot of time dancing with the Belcher the other night. She's *Brendan's* girlfriend, you know." All the guys in the room laughed.

My ears got hot. I started to say, *No, she's not!* but Morgan walked in.

She slipped into her seat without a glance or a word. Something told me this was not going to be a good week at Eastmont Middle.

———

When I got home that afternoon, Dad said he would be taking me to Tae Kwon Do as usual. The bad news was, he was staying.

Since Dad's evening classes had started, he'd just been dropping me off on his way to school, and Khal and his dad would drive me home.

"You're staying?" I said.

"Yeah. Class was cancelled. Is there a problem?" Dad's eyebrows rose.

"Uh. No. *No.* It's just . . . great, you're staying." I escaped to my room to do some homework and spend a little time with Einstein before we had to leave. *What I really should be doing is practicing my forms,* I thought as I searched for Einstein through the glass.

Over the last month, my practice had been slipping. Between having a heavier load of homework, taking care of Einstein, and doing extra chores around the house to earn more allowance for my new bike, I didn't have nearly as much free time as I'd had in elementary school. On top of that, for the last week and a half, Morgan's and my experiment had been in my usual practice space. I couldn't practice in that heat. And the odor, although not totally gagging, didn't exactly make me want to hang out there any longer than I had to. I went in there twice a day for the measurements and got out as fast as I could (without jeopardizing the accuracy of the data, of course).

Then there was the fact that Dad had been so busy with his own homework and his job that he hadn't seemed to notice I wasn't practicing. Without Dad reminding me to practice, well, it was just easy not to. And without practice, I wouldn't be advancing to the next level any time soon.

Each level, or belt color, in Tae Kwon Do has its own *hyung*, or form—a series of blocks, punches, and kicks that students have to memorize and perform convincingly to qualify for the next belt or stripe (the levels between belts). I had six *hyungs* down, although with my lack of practice, some of them had been getting kind of fuzzy, and the most recent one—*Toi-Gye*, which I had to learn before earning my brown stripe—wasn't coming along so well. Only three more *hyungs* and I'd have my first-degree black belt, but lately I just hadn't been motivated.

Master Rickman had even said something to me about putting in more time at home if I wanted to be ready for the brown stripe promotion test. I guessed he could see I wasn't as sharp as usual. As soon as we got to the *dojang* that evening, Dad would see it, too.

———

Inside the *dojang*, I threw my shoes into a cubby and walked over to where Khal stood, his arms folded across his chest. "Hey," I said.

"Hey."

"Why'd you ignore me at school?" I said.

"I didn't ignore you."

"Why didn't you call me back Saturday?"

"I didn't have anything to say."

"What's the big deal?" I asked. "So, some girls wanted to dance with me?"

"*All* the girls. Even some eighth graders!"

I smiled a little. "That was crazy, huh?"

Khal rolled his eyes.

"Anyway, who cares?"

Khal's lips scrunched up on one side of his face. I guessed he did.

Master Rickman came to the front of the room. Khal and I would have to finish this later. We bowed to our teacher. "*Shi jak!*" Master Rickman called out.

The first few *hyungs* were no problem. I'd been doing them for the last couple of years and basically did them on autopilot. The next couple were a little sloppy. When I got to *Toi-Gye*, though, I choked. Like on-a-chicken-bone choked.

Khalfani kicked and punched with precision and confidence. I could tell I was slipping behind and even needed to watch Khal out of the corner of my eye to remember what to do next. I glanced at Dad standing in the back of the room. He was scowling. I punched when I should have blocked. I turned hot all over, like one big exothermic reaction.

We ended with our *ki hap*—"Ha!"—and bowed to Master Rickman, who bowed in return. I went back to my place and sat, feeling Dad's disapproving stare boring into my back. I glanced at his reflection in the big mirror. Yep, still frowning.

At the end of practice, all the students recited together the five tenets of Tae Kwon Do. "Courtesy! Integrity! Perseverance! Self-control! Indomitable spirit!" I shouted the words as loud as I could, hoping Dad could hear my voice above the others.

"Good work, everyone," Master Rickman said, walking over to two younger boys who were horsing around. They reminded me of Khal and me when we had started out two and a half years ago. He put a hand on each of their shoulders, telling them without words to quiet down. He made a few announcements, including reminding us about our annual Friendship Tournament coming up in a month.

Afterwards, Khal and I walked over to Dad. I kneaded my shoulder as if it were sore, even though it felt perfectly fine.

"Looking good, Khalfani," Dad said.

"Thanks, Detective Buckley." Khal looked around. "Did you see my dad?"

"He forgot something at his office. We're taking you home tonight."

"Oh. Okay."

Master Rickman walked over. "Good to see you, Detective Buckley. It's been a while." He and Dad shook hands.

"I've been a little busier than usual."

Master Rickman nodded, then turned to Khal. "Excellent work tonight, Khalfani. You look ready for the next promotion test."

Khal bowed slightly. *"Kam sa ham nida, nim,"* he said. *Thank you, sir.*

"Keep it up and you'll have your black belt by summer."

Khal beamed. "Really?" Then, just as quickly, his face got serious. "What about Brendan?"

"What do you think, Brendan?" Master Rickman asked. "Are you ready for your next promotion exam?"

Dad stood with his arms crossed, staring down at me like the big statue of Paul Bunyan I'd seen online when I was researching my fifth-grade report on Minnesota.

The way I'd fumbled my *hyung*, the answer was obvious. I was *far* from ready. "No, sir," I mumbled.

"Speak up, Brendan," Dad said.

"*No, sir.*"

Dad spoke to Master Rickman. "Unfortunately, between work and going back to school this fall, I haven't been staying on Brendan about practicing." Dad's eyes locked onto mine. "Starting today, however, that will be changing."

"Maybe you'd like to come in Thursday. Put in some extra time," Master Rickman suggested.

"That's a good idea," Dad said. "I'll see if your mom can bring you." Dad had class on Thursday nights, too.

"I can't!" I said quickly. "That's our monthly rock club meeting. I already told Grandpa Ed I'd be there."

Dad's jaw clenched. "We'll talk about it at home. You might need to miss the rock club this month."

I scowled, even though I knew it would only irritate Dad more if he saw my face.

"Thanks," Dad said to Master Rickman, "and again, my apologies. Come on, boys, let's go." Dad turned toward the door.

Khal and I pulled on our shoes and headed to the car. Khal called shotgun. I sat in back. Dad's disappointment pressed down on me—heavy as the bulletproof vest he'd once let me try on.

As we drove to Khal's house, Dad and Khal talked

nonstop—about the Eastmont football team and a case Dad was working on and Dwight David's flexible eyebrows. Dad laughed when he heard what Ms. Manley had done with her eyeballs. I sat there quietly, feeling a million miles away.

Log Entry—Monday, October 8

Morgan called tonight to talk about the experiment. I was glad she didn't bring up the dance. Hopefully now we can get back to focusing on what matters—science.

CHAPTER 15

The next day, I sat at my desk in World Civilizations class, wiping the sweat from the sides of my face. My shower had gotten cut short after PE because of Dwight David. He'd launched a pee stream that went at least six feet and almost hit Herbie Stiles in the head. He had us scrambling to get out as fast as we could—before I had time to rinse my face. So, I was wiping my sweat with my hands.

Morgan waved as she took her seat a couple of aisles away. I waved hi back.

More kids rushed in, including Khal, trying to make it to their seats before the bell. A couple of the guys in the back were entertaining everyone around them with a description of Dwight David's "performance" in the shower. Dwight David sat a few seats to my right, a satisfied smile on his face.

Mrs. Simmons got up from her desk and started to write on the board. Dwight David grinned.

I looked where he was staring. Mrs. Simmons wore a clingy brown dress. She wasn't an overly large woman—just a little plump in her rear end, and just plump enough that the clingy brown material, once it had gotten lodged in her crack from sitting, wasn't coming out again without a little help.

Even as Mrs. Simmons was reaching for her behind, I saw Dwight David's mouth open and his tongue poke out. The moment she pulled on the fabric, he let loose a loud raspberry. A few kids laughed.

She turned with a scowl, but it was directed at all of us, not specifically at Dwight David. Lucky for him she didn't assume he'd made the sound, although she must have known he was the most likely culprit. "All right, settle down. Time to get started." The bell rang and she walked to the door to close it. "Today we're starting a unit on the rise and fall of the Roman Empire. But first, some review." Mrs. Simmons pointed her yardstick to the question on the board: "What are the five components of civilization?"

Lauren stuck her hand up first.

"Yes, Lauren," Mrs. Simmons said.

"Specialized workers."

Mrs. Simmons nodded. She turned to write the answer on the board. Apparently, walking from the door to the board had pulled in the dress again. The wedgie was back. And this wasn't just the rolling hills variety. This was canyon country. A serious *taco* wedgie.

A few of the boys were snickering.

"Cities!" Khal called out. He was holding back a laugh.

"Was there a raised hand to go with that answer?" Mrs. Simmons looked over her shoulder.

Khal raised his hand.

"Yes, Khalfani?"

"Cities."

Mrs. Simmons wrote "cities" on the board. "Excellent. What else?" she asked.

Dwight David raised his hand, looking very serious.

"Yes, Dwight David?"

"Advanced technology."

Mrs. Simmons smiled. "Very *good*, Dwight David." She turned again to write, quickly pulling her dress from her butt, as if she hoped no one would notice if she did it while she was moving.

Dwight David noticed. He blew another loud, wet raspberry.

I couldn't help it. I laughed. So did most everyone else.

Most everyone else with the exception of Mrs. Simmons.

She scanned the classroom with narrowed eyes. "Who did that?" Her gaze landed on Dwight David.

No one moved. I don't think anyone even breathed.

Her eyes continued to roam our faces as if she was waiting for someone to fess up.

I glanced at Dwight David. I could see Khal frowning in my peripheral vision. I looked over my shoulder at him. He pushed out his lips like he was shushing me and shook his head.

Mrs. Simmons suddenly sounded a little too much like the character in a horror movie who turns out to be the psychopath. "I said, who *did* that?"

A few of us squirmed in our seats. She glared at us from behind her desk. "All right, since no one wants to take responsibility for that rude display of behavior, I will hold you all responsible. You will all be receiving a negative interim report for gross lack of respect."

My palms turned clammy. My heart rammed against my rib cage. A negative report for not showing respect? No explanation I could offer would get me out of trouble for that criminal offense. Dad would be totally *ticked*!

I glanced around again. Everyone's lips were stuck shut, except Morgan's, whose mouth hung open as if she couldn't believe what she was hearing.

This was so totally wrong! But if I spoke up, I would be permanently labeled a sellout or a narc or worse. I kept my lips together like everyone else, but I was feeling really hot. I was so hot that if I *did* open my mouth, I was sure flames would come shooting out. And I would shoot them right at that dork, Dwight David.

"Even in the middle of talking about civilization you

can't be civilized," Mrs. Simmons said crossly. "Everyone open your books to page sixty-four and read the section on the Roman Empire. *Silently*. If I hear so much as a peep, you'll be reading your book in the principal's office."

Mrs. Simmons swept her dress beneath her as she took her seat. She nodded toward someone behind me. "Yes, Morgan?"

I craned my neck. Morgan looked nervous, but sort of angry, too. *Oh, no . . . She wouldn't, would she?*

"It was Dwight David," she said softly. She glanced at him, then back at the teacher. Dwight David slumped in his chair.

Mrs. Simmons's chest expanded as she drew in a breath. She exhaled through her nose. "Thank you, Morgan."

Didn't Morgan know what this would do to her reputation? Probably not. She was new to the whole public school thing, after all. I felt sorry for her. But honestly, I was grateful, too. She had just saved all of our skins.

"Let's go, Dwight David." Mrs. Simmons stood and walked Dwight David out the door. I don't think any of us dared to glance below her waistline.

Kids whispered and giggled around me. I looked back at Morgan, but she already had her nose in her book, no doubt reading about the rule of Caesar Augustus. When I looked at Khal, he glanced in Morgan's direction, shook his head, and gave a thumbs-down. I shrugged, trying not to look too glad that I wasn't going to be in trouble with Dad. Even though I was. *Super*glad.

And I'm not exactly sure, but I think I felt happy that Morgan hadn't tried to protect that little goofball. Maybe she didn't like him after all.

CHAPTER 16

Wednesday was our big meeting with the social worker—our "home study"—to make sure our house was clean and safe and that we'd make a good family for some child.

Mom and Dad had already been to the adoption agency's office for one interview, and Mom had had to go to the police department to get fingerprinted for an FBI check. The adoption agency had even run a background check on Dad—it didn't matter that he was a police detective. Gladys and I had wanted to get fingerprinted, too, just because it sounded cool, but Dad said that wouldn't be necessary.

When I got home from school, Gladys was already there. She had insisted on being a part of the in-home visit. "I want that social worker to know this child is going to have a strong, independent black woman as her grandma." Mom had expressed a lot of enthusiasm. Dad had just rolled his eyes and warned her to watch what she said.

"Hi, Gladys," I said, dropping my backpack onto the love seat and plopping down beside it.

"Hello, grandson. How was school?" Gladys sat on the couch with her feet on the coffee table. She wore her fuzzy orange socks and sipped Mountain Dew through the straw in her metal stein. She said the metal kept it colder, which it probably did. I'd have to do an experiment on that sometime.

"Good. Where's Mom and Dad?" I pulled out my lunch leftovers and started munching on tortilla chips.

"Your mom's running around like a turkey with its head cut off, trying to make everything perfect." Gladys pointed to some chip crumbs I'd dropped on the floor. "Better watch out. Last time I saw her, she had the vacuum. You might lose your fingers if you're not careful."

Mom had already vacuumed the night before, every square inch of the house—even the curtains! And she'd asked me to dust, which is my usual chore, but this time I was supposed to dust everything and anything—even the houseplants! She'd promised me an extra five dollars of allowance if I did a really good job, but I would have done a really good job anyway. I didn't want anything, especially not some stupid old dust, to stand in the way of us getting a baby.

I was on my knees picking up crumbs when Mom rushed in. "Gladys, I hope you're prepared to be sonless, because I'm going to *kill* him!" Mom towered over me, choking a vacuum hose with her hand. Her chest and neck were red and the color was spreading quickly. The Momometer was registering a temperature of about semi-livid.

I checked the love seat for crumbs and stood. "Where is he?" I asked.

"I have no idea. I've texted him at least ten times and haven't gotten a response."

I slipped into the kitchen and dumped the crumbs and my crumpled lunch bag into the trash.

Mom's phone chimed. She checked for the message. "He just left the courthouse. That's twenty minutes still—at *best*. Jeez-o-pete!" She yelled at the phone, as if Dad could hear her, "It's going to take you a long time to make up for this one, buster!"

The doorbell rang. The red drained from Mom's face. She stood there, pale and frozen, like an ice pop that's had all the juice sucked out of it.

Gladys sprang into action. She grabbed the vacuum from Mom's hand, shoved it in the closet, and patted Mom's cheeks. "Everything's going to be fine, Kate. Just leave it to me!" Gladys hopped down the stairs to the landing, where she yanked off her fuzzy socks and slipped on her black shoes. Gladys can move when she wants to.

Mom suddenly came to. She hurried down the stairs, getting there just as Gladys opened the door.

"Hello, Mary!" Mom said without a hint of the anger from the minute before. She smoothed her blouse. "Please, come in."

Mary was an older white woman, tall and thin like Gladys, with poofy graying hair that curled away from her face and looked as if it was held in place with about a gallon of hair spray.

"This is my mother-in-law, Gladys Buckley."

"How do you do?" Gladys said, taking the woman's coat and hanging it on the hooks behind her.

"Very well, thank you." Mary looked to where I stood. "You must be Brendan," she said, climbing the stairs.

"Yes, ma'am." I shook her hand, firmly so she'd know I was confident enough to handle a new baby, but not so firmly that she'd think I was too rough for him or her.

"It's a pleasure finally to meet you." Mary looked around. "What a lovely home."

"Thank you," Mom said, rushing to join us. "Please have a seat. Can I get you something to drink—tea, cranberry juice?"

"Mountain Dew?" Gladys added, moving to the coffee table and raising her stein.

At least the social worker would know Gladys wasn't drinking *beer* through that straw. I grabbed my backpack from the love seat so Mary could sit.

Mary smiled. "I'm fine for now." She glanced around and drew her briefcase onto her lap. "Is Sam here?"

Mom's face tensed. "Um . . . no. I'm really sorry. He got caught up in court." Mom motioned me to the couch. "But he'll be here shortly," she added quickly.

I set my pack inside the entryway to the kitchen and went and sat between Gladys and Mom, who perched stiffly with her hands clasped between her knees.

"No problem. Things happen." Mary pulled out a clipboard. "We can start with the home inspection." She made a note of something. Was she writing down that Dad was late? Mom's nervousness must have been catching, because I was starting to feel it, too.

Mary rose and went to the front window. She checked behind the curtains. "Good. Cords are safely stored away." She looked down at the wall. "Covers on the outlets . . . You have these in every room, I take it."

"Yes," Mom said. Her leg had started to jiggle. She stood and followed Mary into the kitchen.

"All knives are being kept in secured cabinets?" Mary opened and shut a drawer.

"Absolutely," Mom said. Dad had spent several hours the previous week installing specialized latches on practically every cabinet in our house. They could only be released with this one magnetic key. I had started off helping him, but after the second one he'd told me he'd better just do it himself. I heard him cursing the things from my room.

Later, he told Mom the instructions hadn't said anything about needing an engineering degree. Really, the latches didn't require intellect to install as much as patience, which Dad can be short on. He's plenty smart, even if he sometimes talks as if he's not.

We trailed along like tourists getting a tour of our own house. In the bathroom, Mary turned on the hot water in the tub. She flushed the toilet.

"If you're concerned about backups, there's no need to worry," Gladys said. "I've seen that toilet handle some hefty loads."

I laughed. Mom pinched her lips tightly and gave us both a good stare.

"What?" Gladys said with eyes wide. "It's a natural process. Nothing to be ashamed of."

Mary had produced a thermometer from somewhere and held it under the running bathwater. "Is your water heater set for under one-twenty?"

"Yes. One-oh-nine, I think. We try to conserve wherever we can," Mom said, following Mary down the hall. "Not to the point of discomfort, of course. We'll spare no expense to make sure our children are healthy and well cared for."

Mary turned and stopped abruptly, causing a collision between Mom, Gladys, and me. "Kate, please." She rested her hand on Mom's arm. "*Relax*. This is all just a formality, really. Of course I know your home will be a wonderfully welcome place for another child."

Mom laughed, still not her regular bird-on-a-spring-day laugh, but after that she seemed to calm down a little.

Mary poked her head into the first room on the left.

"That's the nursery . . . assuming our new child will be an infant." Mom had spent hours cleaning out the boxes Grandpa Ed had brought over, full of Grandma DeBose's things that he thought Mom might like to have. All that was in there now were the white crib and dresser Mom had bought off Craigslist a couple of weeks ago, a framed bedtime prayer that Grandma DeBose had done in needlepoint, and the rocking chair she'd intended Mom to have when I was born. Mom had painted the walls a light green and put up a border covered with teddy bears and pink roses. Roses had been Grandma DeBose's favorite flower. The room actually looked pretty nice. But I hoped, for the baby's sake, she was a *she* and not a he.

"It's lovely," Mary said.

"Thank you," Mom said.

My room was next. Mom had done an army inspection that morning before I'd left for school. I showed Mary my rock and mineral collection, my mobile of the solar system, which I'd made myself, and my neatly folded purple belt. "A big brother who knows martial arts. That's a plus," Mary said, making more notes.

Mom smiled and nodded at me from behind the woman.

I had saved Einstein for last. Fortunately, he was basking, so we could get a good view. "Does he ever come out of the tank?" Mary asked.

"Only when I clean it, which I have to do about once a month. I put him in this temporary holder for that." I held up the small plastic case. I figured she didn't need to know I'd only done it once so far, or that anoles are known as master escape artists.

"Oh, I see." Mary checked off something else on her list.

"Will having a lizard be a problem?" Mom sounded worried again.

"He's totally harmless," I added.

"Unless you're a cricket or a mealworm," Gladys said.

"He's parasite-free," Mom said over Gladys's chuckling. "We had him checked by a vet when we bought him."

"Lizards are fine, especially one so small." Mary peered into the tank. She waggled her finger at Einstein as if he were the little baby. "And so *cute*."

We made our way around Mom and Dad's bedroom, where Mary wanted to see the exact place Dad kept his handgun locked away and gave extensive warnings about how it could never, ever, for any reason, be left unlocked and unattended.

"Believe me, there is no *way* Sam would ever compromise his children's safety with that thing. If it weren't for his job, I wouldn't even allow it in our house. . . ."

Mom continued talking, but I was lost in thought

about something she had said. *His* children's *safety*. Dad and Mom were going to have more than just me soon. I knew it was something they really wanted, especially Mom, and I knew this new kid wouldn't replace me—Mom had told me so a dozen times, at least—but still, it gave me a strange feeling to know I wasn't going to be an only child anymore.

I'd been memorizing the periodic table of chemical elements, since elements are what make up minerals. Mom, Dad, and I had always been a family of three, like lithium (Li), number three on the periodic table. Three protons in an enclosed, complete atom. But after this baby came, we would be four. Beryllium. What would it be like to be Be?

Mom, Gladys, and Mary chatted as they left the room. I followed, quiet from all my thoughts. We were on the stairs to the basement when Dad rushed in.

I was between Mom and the front door. She turned and gave Dad a major stink-eye. She held it just long enough for Dad to know she was serious, but not so long that it got embarrassing. "Good timing, dear. We're almost through with the inspection, then Mary wants to speak with us in the living room. Meet us there?" She cocked her head and gave him a forced-looking smile.

"Sure. Great. My apologies, Mary." Dad stepped past Mom and me and reached down the stairs to shake Mary's hand. "I had to testify today, and the hearing went long."

"My son is a detective in the Tacoma Police Department," Gladys said. "A very important job."

"Yes. We've talked all about it," Mary said, smiling. "Take your time, Sam. Now, let's see the basement." She turned and continued downstairs.

Mom and I had agreed that we'd handle the bottles of manure very matter-of-factly and not try to hide anything. Of course, she'd hoped the in-home visit would happen after Morgan's and my experiment was completed, but Mary had had an opening and Mom didn't want to delay our application.

Mary inspected the laundry room, bathroom, and Dad's study area first. Finally, we headed to the rec room. I scooted past Mary. "Here, let me get the light," I said. I opened the door. Intense heat and the smell of fermenting manure smacked us in the face. I flipped the switch.

"What's going on in *here*?" Mary's voice had taken on an edge of concern.

Mom started to speak, but I jumped in. "A friend and I are conducting an experiment on alternative fuel sources. Our science class is participating in a national science competition."

"Really?" Mary sounded interested.

"I know this is probably off the charts against what's allowable," Mom said, "but all of it will be gone in a week and a half, tops. Right, Bren?" Mom looked at me. I nodded.

"Well, that's good, because honestly"—Mary sniffed

the air—"you're right, Kate. This all seems a bit . . . toxic. What's in these bottles?"

I spoke up again. "Rotting vegetables, banana, some purified water . . . manure." I slipped in the last word as casually as I could, remembering how I had literally slipped in it a couple of weeks before.

"Manure! Oh, *no.* We could never approve a placement with this in your house."

"It's definitely temporary," I said, "although it's possible that people could generate a lot of energy for their homes with these kinds of digesters. On a much larger scale, of course."

"Digesters?" Mary said.

I explained the science behind anaerobic digestion and biogas production as we walked back to the living room. Mary nodded, seeming very interested in everything I said, which of course encouraged me to keep talking. And I had plenty to say after studying the subject for the past few weeks.

Dad walked in and joined Mom on the couch. Gladys was in the armchair. I was in the middle of telling Mary about a dairy farm in Minnesota that generated enough electricity with their nine hundred and thirty cows' manure to power their own farm *and* eighty additional homes in the area.

"Is that so?" Mary said. She turned to Mom and Dad. "I'm so impressed with your son! I've learned some things today I'd never even heard of before."

"Oh, yeah," Dad said. "Brendan comes up with some interesting ideas, all right."

Except the way he said it, *interesting* sounded more like *strange*.

"We're very proud of him," Mom said, beckoning me over. I went and sat on the other side of her from Dad. I sank back into the couch, feeling as if I'd done something wrong.

Mary put her clipboard on her lap and clicked on her pen. "So, tell me, Buckley family, what strengths do you see yourselves having to offer another child?"

"I'll tell you one thing that's for sure," Gladys piped up. "My new grandbaby's going to know how to ride public transportation. Riding the bus teaches you life skills—self-assertiveness, money and time management, reading maps, dealing with strangers—and you *do* meet some strange ones. I take the bus everywhere—the Super Mall, my podiatrist, Muckleshoot Casino—"

"*Mama.* We're not here to talk about your bus exploits." Dad turned to Mary. "Sorry."

"I think it's great that you want to be so involved in your new grandchild's life, Mrs. Buckley."

"Thank you." Gladys crossed her legs, folded her arms, and leaned back in the armchair, giving Dad a "so there" look.

"We will give the child love and absolute acceptance," Mom said.

"Along with consistency and discipline," Dad said.

"My dad made the rules clear, and he expected us to follow them. I didn't always like it at the time, but it kept me on a good path." He eyed me across Mom, but I avoided his gaze.

It was hard for me to imagine Grampa Clem being as strict as Dad always painted him. Grampa Clem had never raised his voice or said a sharp word to me, ever.

They continued talking about how Mom and Dad ran the house. When Mary asked how I felt about the way things were, I said everything was great. The only things that could have been better were if I got a little more for allowance and if Mom bought sugared cereal every once in a while, which made Mary laugh. They moved on to discussing whether they'd get time off from work when the placement happened and Dad's plans to finish his degree in the next year.

My thoughts drifted to the science contest. Morgan and I had just walked onstage to receive our first-place medals when Mary's voice broke in. "And Brendan, what are you looking forward to about having a sister, assuming your family gets a little girl?"

I was glad she hadn't asked me if I knew how to change a diaper, or if I thought all babies were cute, because I didn't—in either case.

I sat and thought for a minute. I pictured Grampa Clem and me standing side by side on the pier with our poles in the water, quiet for the most part, except when I had a question, and then Grampa Clem would answer me, and I always knew he was telling me the truth.

"Taking her fishing," I said. "And telling her the truth about stuff."

Mary nodded. Her eyes smiled.

"Oh—and teaching her the periodic table of elements." We all laughed, even though I was dead serious.

"Of course," Mary said. "Every girl should know the periodic table of elements." She snapped her briefcase shut. "Next time you hear from me, I expect to be delivering some very happy news."

Mom sucked in her breath and clapped her hands together. She hugged me so tight a little water even popped out of my eyes.

CHAPTER 17

Mom was so ecstatic about passing the home study, she either forgot about or just overlooked Dad's being late. She got on the phone as soon as Mary left to tell Grandpa Ed the good news.

While Mom talked to Grandpa Ed, Gladys added her commentary. "They'll put you behind the wheel of a car or hand you a lethal weapon with less scrutiny than what we got today. I'm telling you, Sam, any Jane, John, or JuLinda can have a baby, and they don't have to go through everything short of a body-cavity search. But as soon as you say you want to *adopt* . . ." Gladys raised her voice. "Kate, did you tell Rock they even checked your crapper? Oh, and what about Mary's face when she saw those bottles of dung! Tell him about *that*, Kate!" Gladys hooted.

"Mama, please. Quiet down already." Dad left the room. I stayed to be entertained.

After dinner, Dad took Gladys home. When he returned, Mom and I were in the living room talking about what life would be like with a baby. Dad perched on the love seat. "Hey, I keep forgetting to ask. Can you take Brendan to Tae Kwon Do tomorrow night?"

"You said we were going to talk about it!" Now it was *my* turn to get mad at Dad.

"Wait a minute. What's going on?" Mom looked back and forth between us.

"Tomorrow is the monthly rock club meeting," I said.

"Master Rickman thinks Brendan needs some extra practice. And so do I," said Dad. "I told him he needed to be in the *dojang* tomorrow."

"You *told* me we'd talk about it at home."

Mom frowned. "Couldn't he put in an extra practice next week, Sam? The rock club's just once a month."

"The rock club's not going anywhere," Dad said.

"And Tae Kwon Do *is*?" I said. "It's only been around like a *thousand years!*" I knew I was "giving him lip," as he called it, but I didn't care. He was going back on his word. He'd probably never intended to discuss it at all.

"Do you want to get your black belt or not?" he asked.

I did, but I had other interests, too. Couldn't he understand that? Probably not. His whole life revolved around being a police officer. "Yes, but—"

"Then you need to earn it, and that means putting in the time. You've got to see it through, Brendan."

"I *will*. I'll go to the studio twice next week, like Mom said. I'll go twice a week *every* week except for the weeks we have the rock club meeting, if that's what you want." I spit the words.

Mom's mouth was all bunched up, as if she were trying to keep herself from speaking. I didn't understand why. She knew Dad was being too hard about this.

"Fine," Dad said.

Somehow it didn't seem fine.

Later, after we'd all gone to bed, I came out of my room to get a drink from the bathroom. Mom and Dad's bedroom door was cracked. "What was going on between you and Brendan earlier?" I heard Mom ask.

I froze in my tracks.

"He just needs to learn, that's all."

"Learn what?"

"If he wants to achieve certain goals, he needs to do the work to get there."

"Brendan works *very* hard, Sam. You know that." Silence. "Anyway, *is* a black belt his goal? Or is it just yours for him?"

I stayed as still as I could. I wanted to hear what Dad had to say.

"Not this again. Brendan wants his black belt. He's said so a hundred times. He said so tonight."

"He *wants* your approval."

"All sons want their dads' approval."

Another long silence. I didn't know how much longer I could stand there. My tensed legs had started to twitch. And what would I do if one of my parents suddenly appeared at the door?

Finally, Dad spoke again. "Look, something's causing him to fall behind in his practice. Personally, I think he's spending too much time on this science stuff—the rock thing with your dad, the experiment in our basement, even that lizard. . . ."

My heart started racing.

"Too much time on science?" Mom sounded shocked. "How in the world could you think that's a problem?"

I had known Dad wasn't that excited about our manure experiment, and he hadn't shown much interest in my new hobby of rock and mineral collecting, either. But the way he was talking now, calling it "stuff" and saying I was spending too much time on it, made me feel like I was doing something wrong again. Like when he'd told the social worker my ideas were *interesting*. Maybe it wasn't just my ideas he thought were strange. Maybe he thought *I* was strange, too, for being so into science.

My heart still pounded. I knew I shouldn't be listening, but I couldn't help it. I wanted to know what else Dad would say.

"When are you going to accept the fact that your son is wired differently from you?" Mom asked.

"I do accept it! I know Brendan is smarter than I was at his age."

"That's *not* what I said." Mom's voice punched like fists.

"Smarter. Differently wired. Whatever. The point is he's good at school, but there are other things that matter just as much, if not more."

"Things that matter more than school? What are you talking about?"

"I'm talking about real-world experience. Like the things you learn from sports. Discipline, being a team player, getting back up when you're knocked down . . . the kind of toughness you need to get through life."

"I don't want Brendan to be *tough*. Courageous, strong . . . fine. But he doesn't need to be tough. Toughness is overrated."

"Not for boys, it's not."

Mom blew out a long, loud breath. "I thought you'd finally come around to your dad's position—his whole emphasis on education, finishing your degree."

"Sure, I'm getting my degree, but not everyone's going to get straight As. My dad punished me for not being like my older brother."

"He pushed you because he wanted you to have options—opportunities he didn't have."

"Yeah, well, I hated the pressure."

"Well, then don't do the same thing to Brendan.

Don't overlook what he's good at because you want him to be good at something else."

"I'm trying to *help* him."

"Just like your dad was trying to help you."

"You don't understand, Kate. Boys like him—"

"What do you mean, *boys like him?*" Mom's voice jabbed again.

"You know what I mean. The studious kids. The eggheads. They get beat down. I'm just looking out for his own good."

The room got quiet. I had heard enough. I slunk back to my room. *Boys like him,* I kept hearing Dad say. *Boys like him get beat down.* And what was an egghead, anyway?

I went to my computer and pulled up an online dictionary.

"Egghead: an intellectual. Synonyms: geek, nerd."

Nerd? The word knocked the wind out of me. Then I imagined that Dad was the wind and I was a windmill. If he stopped blowing, I was nothing. Without his support, how would I ever be all I was supposed to be?

I made a new entry in my log. A lot had happened today, but I only had one thing on my mind.

Log Entry—Wednesday, October 10

Dad thinks I'm a science-nerd wimp. Am I?

CHAPTER 18

I went to the rock club meeting, and it was all right, although the whole time the speaker talked I had a hard time not thinking about the fight I'd had with Dad, or the fact that I'd committed to attending two practices a week at the *dojang* indefinitely.

Things got better when we went into the lapidary shop. My mind got completely focused on learning how to use the polishing belts.

Grandpa Ed gave me a pair of protective goggles and half of a thunder egg he'd sawn in two; then he showed me how to hold the flat surface against the wet belt, moving it slightly to keep it even, checking it now and then to see if it was ready for the next grade of sandpaper. I could have stayed there all night polishing that stone. As it was, I only got about halfway done, but Grandpa Ed said we could come back any time I wanted to work on it. He had the keys to the building, after all.

Morgan had been there, too, of course. Her reputation at school didn't seem to be suffering too much. The last couple of days, I'd even overheard a few kids come up to her and thank her for getting them out of trouble. Apparently, Dwight David's clowning around hadn't improved social status at Eastmont Middle.

Khal couldn't be swayed, however. He maintained that Dwight David had acted as our fall guy.

"But he brought it on himself," I insisted the next night when Khal was at our house. I'd invited him over to hang out, eat dinner, maybe watch a movie.

"We all laughed," Khal said, "so we were all in on the joke, and we *all* should have covered for him."

I just didn't get what Khal saw in that kid.

"Really, that was so not cool, what your girlfriend did."

"She's not my girlfriend."

"Right. She's just your *science* partner." Khal looked into Einstein's tank, but Einstein was hiding out somewhere.

"Did *you* want to get a negative interim? Your stepmom would've had you cleaning the bathrooms with your toothbrush."

"Yeah, and then made me brush my teeth with it." He laughed. "Just fooling. Still, she shouldn't have ratted him out like that."

I grabbed the water bottle and pumped a few squirts into the tank. "Why would you want to take a hit for him, anyway? He's a clown."

"Exactly. He's funny. Plus, he's really good at building things."

Khal and Dwight David were building a pneumatic launcher for the contest. They would video themselves launching it and submit that as part of their entry. I'd questioned him about how a launcher would make the world better exactly. "I'm not sure yet," he'd said. "But I know it will make the world a whole lot *cooler*!" I assumed he wasn't referring to global warming.

When Dad had heard about Khal's project earlier that evening, he'd gotten excited—and given Khal an answer to my question. "Our department just purchased some pneumatic launchers for search and rescue. You can shoot grappling hooks almost a hundred yards, set climbing ropes to scale buildings, launch buoys and life preservers to people stranded in deep waters— it's like something right out of *Batman*!" He'd slapped Khal on the back. "Let me know how it turns out, buddy."

I'd stood by silently.

I put the water bottle back under the table. Einstein still hadn't appeared. I'd thought the water droplets might get him moving around.

"You should come with me to Dwight David's house sometime. His grandma makes these egg roll things called *lumpia*. They're awesome. I could eat a hundred of them. Did you know his family's Filipino?"

I shook my head. Actually, I had wondered if Dwight David was mixed like me. Not black and white, but some kind of mix. His skin was just as brown, but his jet-black hair was totally straight. Even with his buzz cut, you could tell that. I'd never asked him, though, because I know how it feels to get asked that question—like being an unknown species someone's trying to classify.

"They're the best. They totally make you feel like you're part of the family. And they're loud and crazy. There's always people at their house whenever I go over there, and they act like they're all related, even if they're not." Khal sat in my desk chair and spun around. "His dad's been fighting in Afghanistan for the last two years."

"Two years?" And I thought *my* dad had been gone a lot lately.

"Yeah. Being a military kid, he's moved around a lot. I think when he acts goofy he's just trying to get people to like him."

Maybe Khal was right. I supposed I could try to be a little nicer.

Khal pointed to the tank. "There's no lizard in there, man. You're just messing with me."

"I'm not! He's in there. He's just shy. And arboreal."

"Ar-boree-what?"

"He likes to hang out in trees and bushes. Hide behind leaves. Come back tomorrow morning at eight. Feeding time. He always comes out then."

"Can't we feed him now?"

"He's not supposed to get fed too much. Besides, I'm training him. I feed him at the same time, every other . . ." I glanced at the clock on my desk: 7:03! *Shoot.* I was three minutes late. Our two weeks of measuring the balloons would be over tomorrow night—I couldn't mess things up now. "I'll be back in a minute," I said, squeezing between Khal and my desk and opening the top drawer.

"Where are you going?"

"To measure my gas production." I grabbed a pen, my science notebook, the string I wrapped around the balloons to mark their circumferences, and my ruler.

"*Gas* production? Oh, yeah."

I hurried out the door.

"You should see a doctor about that!" Khal shouted. "It sounds kind of serious! You want me to get you some *Rolaids?*"

I rushed downstairs into the rec room and started to measure. Morgan had come over a couple of times to check the experiment's progress and take pictures with her camera. The last time, we had moved the bottles apart—very carefully—to allow for the balloon growth. The first bottle was now only a few feet from the door.

I wrapped the string around the last balloon and recorded the measurement. Then I scanned the chart, looking for patterns. The balloons on the manure-banana and manure-veggie bottles had slowed in their production, but the balloons on the manure-only bottles were bigger than ever. The biggest one had a diameter of thirty-four centimeters. (Mr. H had shown us how to calculate diameters from circumferences.) It was as big as a watermelon!

When I was done, I stood back and admired the bottles one last time. We had done it. We had made methane. *Blue ribbon, here we come*. I turned off the light and closed the door.

A huge scream came from somewhere above me. "Aaahhhh!"

I bounded up the stairs. Around the corner. Down the hall.

Khal burst from my room and slammed into me. We both fell to the ground. "He bit me! He bit me!" He sat up, clutching his hand.

Mom appeared from her room. "What happened? What's wrong?" She sounded panicked.

"You took Einstein out?" I yelled.

I heard Dad's footsteps behind me. "What's going on?"

Mom pulled Khal up and started down the hall. I pushed past them into my room. The tank lid was on the ground. "Einstein!" I moved leaves. I lifted his fake bark.

He was gone! If anything happened to my lizard, Khal would be finding himself a new best friend, *pronto*. Dwight David could have him.

A small brown streak shot past me out the door. "Einstein!" I ran down the hall after him.

Mom and Khal sat on the love seat, where she was inspecting his finger. He pointed with his free hand. "Over there!"

Einstein perched on the ledge that separated the living room from the stairwell, as if he were looking to see who was coming in the front door.

I froze. Einstein wouldn't jump, would he?

Khal inched his way toward my lizard.

"Wait," I said. "He's really stressed. That's what it means when he turns brown."

Dad came up behind me holding a bottle of hydrogen peroxide. "Brendan, you had better get that thing back in its tank," he said. "It can't just be running around our house."

"They run around people's houses in Florida," I said, trying to move my mouth as little as possible. I didn't want to startle Einstein into bolting again.

"Brendan, we could have a baby any day," Mom said. "We can't have a lizard on the loose!"

Dad started toward the stairs. "I think I've still got some traps in the garage from that time we had a mouse."

"No!" I shouted, holding him back.

Einstein darted over the ledge, down the wall, and

across the top of the doorframe. "He's headed to the basement!"

Khal caught up to me on the stairs. He grabbed my shoulder. "I'm really sorry, man. I didn't know they were so fast."

I shrugged him off and kept moving. "You shouldn't have tried to take him out."

"I know, I know. I'm sorry." Khal's feet pounded down the stairs behind me.

I headed toward Dad's makeshift study. Maybe Einstein would be drawn to the light of the computer screen.

"I'll look this way," Khal said. He ran in the opposite direction—toward the rec room, where the space heater had been on for the last two weeks. That was where Einstein would go. Not to the light. To the heat!

I turned the corner as Khal plowed into the dark room.

"Where's the light switch in here, man? It's pitch—"

Thud.

The bottles!

I lunged for the light switch. Khal had run right into the two-liters! One bottle crashed into the next, setting off a chain reaction. They looked like dominoes falling in slow motion, one after the other. The liquid sloshed against the sides. The balloons bounced on the ground. I held my breath, hoping, *hoping*, *HOPING*, that the duct tape would hold.

"Don't just stand there!" I yelled. I grabbed the first one and set it upright. The balloon no longer stood straight but lolled to the side. *Dang it, Khal!*

Khal scrambled to reach another tipping bottle before it fell, but his feet got caught in the tangle of our ruined experiment and he stumbled. His knee landed, hard, right in the middle of one of the fallen two-liters. The balloon shot from the end. Brown, chunky water spewed everywhere. A *much* stronger stench than before filled the room. We could have been standing in a cattle pen at the state fair, it smelled so bad. Except it was worse.

"I think it got on me!" Khal's face was frozen in a grimace. He held his arms stiffly in front of him. He looked like a Neolithic caveman discovered in some ice.

Dad appeared in the doorway. His eyes scanned the room as if he were seeing a crime scene for the first time. His jaw bulged. His biceps strained against his sleeves. "Clean it up."

"But I still haven't found—"

"Clean it *all* up. And get it out of here. *Tonight.*" He turned and walked out.

The blood behind my eyes pulsed so hard that the room pulsed, too.

Khal started putting the bottles on their ends.

I crouched near the portable space heater. There he was, my anole, sitting on the carpet between the heater's wheels. His green color was returning in patches.

I knew I only had one chance. I barely breathed as my hand shot beneath the heater. I felt his fragile body in my grasp. I hoped I hadn't squeezed him too hard. I held him between my thumb and first finger, as Morgan had done, and talked to him quietly. "I got you, boy. It's okay. Everything's going to be okay."

But really, I wasn't so sure.

It had taken Khal and me a solid three hours to clean up the rec room after the disaster. We'd found specks of manure as far away as the dartboard on the opposite wall from where the two-liter had fired, which, after I got over being mad, I admitted to Khal had been pretty awesome. We'd dubbed it the "poop cannon." He'd called his parents to explain and ended up spending the night. So he got to watch Einstein eat crickets after all.

Mom had turned the crisis into an opportunity, as she liked to say, by convincing Dad it was the perfect chance to get rid of the old, shaggy green carpet and replace it with fake wood flooring.

We'd taken the bottles outside and dumped the contents into the flower beds, just like the last time we'd done an experiment in two-liters. Only this time, I was confident that what we were dumping would help the plants grow and not turn them brown.

All in all, everything had turned out all right in the end.

Even things with the experiment were going to be okay. That Monday, in science, Mr. Hammond assured Morgan and me that thirteen days of measurements were enough to qualify as a valid experiment and we should go ahead and write up our report for submission to the contest. Applications were due the first week of November, just a couple of weeks away.

"That's great!" Morgan said. I breathed a sigh of relief.

We left Mr. H's class, headed toward the lunchroom. Morgan was being unusually quiet, and it was starting to feel awkward. I was about to say "See you later" when she blurted out, "Do you want to write up the final report together? You could come over to my house this time. For dinner, maybe."

My face scrunched, as involuntarily as my heart jumping around in my chest.

Morgan's cheeks turned hot pink. She spoke quickly and her eyes darted around. "Never mind. Dumb idea. Uh . . . I'll write something up and email it. We can discuss it over the phone. Bye!"

I grabbed her arm. "No. Wait. I want . . ."

She turned and looked at me hopefully.

I just couldn't get the words out of my mouth. "I mean, that would be great if you wrote up a preliminary report. I can give you my notebook with all the measurements."

"Oh. Okay." Her smile drooped, like the balloons after they'd gotten knocked to the ground.

"It's just, the only extra thing I really have time for in the next couple of weeks is Tae Kwon Do," I said, trying to cover for myself. "I've got a promotion test this Saturday, and our big annual tournament is the Saturday after that." I didn't tell her that I had to be ready so I could prove I wasn't a science-nerd wimp. "I'll definitely help with the final report."

"Sure. No problem. You did all the measurements, after all. And the cleanup." She smiled a little. "Sorry about that."

I shrugged. "Wasn't *your* fault."

"I know. But still . . ." Her face perked up. "Hey, could I come to your tournament?"

My heart started jumping around again. "I guess. If you really want to."

"I do! Get me the data before school's out, okay? See you later!" She bounced off toward the lunchroom. I hung back, trying to get my pulse to chill out.

Morgan was coming to see me compete in the annual tournament. I had better be ready. I no longer had just Dad to impress.

Khal and I got our brown stripes today. Big relief. Brown stands for the color of the ground and is supposed to mean that we are "rooted firmly" in our practice of Tae Kwon Do.

Dad got to the *dojang* just in time to see me perform. He had to rush from work to make it. Dad seemed happy, and he and Mom took me to Dairy Queen afterward to celebrate.

Master Rickman told us once that when martial arts first started, there was only one color of belt— white. Over many years of hard training, a student's belt would get darker from all the sweat, dirt, and blood until it turned black. That's how the whole idea of black belts got started. Black is for the ones who have suffered the most. After this past week, my belt is definitely sweatier and dirtier. No blood yet, though.

Can't write any more—my arms are killing me from all the punches I've been doing.

CHAPTER 20

The morning of the Friendship Tournament, I got up early. Kids and adults from studios all over Washington and Oregon would be at the Tacoma Y to compete.

Over breakfast, Dad gave me pointers for the tournament. I nodded a bunch and said yeah a few times, but what I was really thinking was how Dad was showing way more interest in *this* competition than the other one I was in.

I chugged my orange juice, then headed to my room to give Einstein his two crickets and one of the wax worms Grandpa Ed had brought over the other day.

The last thing I did was put on my *do bok*. My purple belt now had a nice brown stripe on it. I had thought a lot about the argument I'd heard my parents having and I'd decided: Getting my black belt *was* important to me. It wasn't just my dad's goal. It was my own—for myself. I had worked hard for my brown stripe and I had earned it. At the tournament, I would prove I deserved it.

On our way to picking up Gladys, we passed Shari's Restaurant. After the tournament, we'd go there to have breakfast for dinner, like always. Only this time, Grandpa Ed would be with us. He was even skipping a rock club expedition to be there. He said he couldn't miss his grandson doing kung fu. I didn't tell him kung fu is Chinese and what I do is Korean. I was just glad he was coming. It was going to be a great day.

We pulled into Gladys's parking lot, past the sign that read WELCOME TO BRIGHTON FIELDS — WHERE LIFE IS IN FULL BLOOM. "But withering quickly," Gladys liked to add. It was a nice day, not too cold. Red and orange leaves glowed like fire against the gray sky.

Gladys waited on the bench out front. *Oh, brother.* She waved her big foam finger. We pulled up and Mom got in the backseat. Gladys got in front. "Ready to crack some skulls?" She snapped her seat belt into place.

"Brendan's school of Tae Kwon Do is noncontact, Mama." Dad waited while Gladys took a swig of bright blue drink from one of her two Gatorade bottles.

"I say we liven things up a bit. What do you say, Brendan?" She looked at me over her shoulder.

I glanced at Dad. "I . . . uh . . ."

"Oh, lighten up, you two! I'm just having a little fun." Gladys passed me the neon yellow Gatorade. "To keep those electro-thingamajigs balanced for peak performance. But I'm sure you know all about that, Mr. Science Genius."

I shrugged and looked out the window. I didn't need Gladys highlighting my nerdy science side right now, especially in front of Dad. Today, I was Brendan Buckley, Tae Kwon Do brown-stripe warrior.

———

The gym was already swarming with people. Most of them wore *do boks* just like mine. The cool thing about tournaments is that you see people of all ages wearing all the different colors of belts. There are adults wearing white belts and kids, some even younger than me, wearing black belts.

First, we went to the judges' table. Master Rickman checked me in. "Here's the schedule. Your forms competition will be in Ring Three around eleven. The *kyepka* will be after that." Breaking boards had become one of my favorite things to do.

I scanned the listings. Gladys read over my shoulder. All the events would be held in this one gym, in six different rings separated only by invisible lines and people waiting their turns to compete. Tournaments were always crowded like this, but I never got used to it. As usual, I'd have to work hard to stay focused.

"What about sparring?" Dad asked.

"I'm guessing junior purple belts will start around one—in Ring One."

Dad nodded. "All right. Good. Brendan, you'll have to watch your food intake. Keep it light."

"Khalfani is around here somewhere." Master Rickman looked out into the gym. "Over there." He pointed. Khal was practicing kicks and punches with his dad.

Gladys held up her plastic seat cushion. "I'm going to find my bony behind a spot near the front, if I still can." The few rows of bleachers were filling up quickly.

I glanced at Master Rickman. Did Gladys have to go and mention her behind in front of my teacher?

"Start stretching, Bren," Dad said. "I'll take your stuff to the bleachers, then join you." He took my coat and the Gatorade and followed Mom and Gladys.

I wound my way around small groups of kids and adults doing their warm-ups. The sounds of talking and laughing bounced around the gym.

Everyone wore the same patches on their *do boks*, no matter where their studio, because even though we all belonged to different *dojangs*, we were all a part of Master Kim's school of Tae Kwon Do. We had the U.S. flag on our right shoulders, the Korean flag on our left shoulders, and a red circle patch on our chests that said KIM'S TAE KWON DO. Master Kim had started his school, like, a hundred years ago or something.

I loved hearing the *swish-swish* of my *do bok* as I walked, and how it made me feel to wear it. *Strong.*

Whoever invented that Shout stuff—now, that guy

(*or girl*, I heard Morgan's voice say) was a science genius. The cow-poop stain from the fair was so faint it was basically unnoticeable. The only brown on my *do bok* from now on would be my stripe, and eventually, a belt.

I pulled back my shoulders and raised my chin. *I am a brown-stripe warrior*, I thought. *Courageous, self-controlled, indomitable.*

I passed a judge in his black belt uniform. Black belts' *do boks* have black piping along the edges of the jackets and pants, and Korean lettering on the backs. One day, not too long from now, I would wear that *do bok*.

I was about to walk up to Khal and his dad when I heard my name. "Brendan!" Morgan stood under the basketball hoop, waving like a maniac. I glanced over at Khal, but if he'd noticed Morgan or me, I couldn't tell. I ducked my head and sauntered over. If Khal asked, I hadn't invited her—she'd invited herself. Anyway, the tournament was free and open to the public. Anyone could come.

"Hi," I said. My voice came out kind of deep, like one of those R & B singers on Dad's oldies-but-goodies CDs. My throat tightened. I coughed a couple of times to make sure I'd sound like myself when I spoke again.

"Hi! Did I miss anything?" Morgan smiled her big metal-and-glitter smile.

"It hasn't even started yet."

"Oh, right." She looked around. "I just wanted to be sure. I really, *really* didn't want to miss anything."

"You didn't." I was sweating like crazy under my *do bok* and I hadn't even done a single kick. Just a small case of pretournament nerves, I told myself. *Don't lose your Kool-Aid, man.* "Where are your parents?"

"They dropped me off and went over to Lowe's. They love that place. That's like their idea of a great date—"

I nearly swallowed my tongue when she said the word *date*.

"—dinner at Five Guys Burgers and Fries and a couple of hours strolling the aisles at Lowe's, checking out the latest in bathroom décor and refrigerator technology. I think it makes them feel like they're making progress on the house remodel they've been talking about since we moved here."

My mouth had dried up like a slug on hot cement.

"I guess I'll go find a seat," Morgan said, finally. "I'll be cheering for you."

"That's okay," I said quickly. Now the saliva poured in like Niagara Falls. "You don't need to cheer." I gulped down the excess spit. How embarrassing would it be to slobber right then? "I mean, you can, but maybe do it silently."

Morgan nodded eagerly. "Of course. I don't want to throw you off."

"Right. Gladys and my mom are over there if you want to sit with them."

"Sure!" Morgan smiled again.

Why had I suggested she sit with *Gladys*? My

grandmother would love having the opportunity to tell a girl all kinds of embarrassing things from when I was a baby. Like the time I stuck a Cheerio up my nose and they couldn't figure out why I wouldn't stop digging up there—until it finally popped out . . . two days later.

"Where are they?"

I didn't need to point out Gladys. She stood waving her gigantic #1 FAN finger.

Morgan giggled. "Oh, I see her! See you later." Morgan's face suddenly bumped against mine, and her lips brushed my cheek. "Good luck." She hurried off.

It felt as if someone had cranked up the heat to a hundred and two. Had Morgan just kissed me on the cheek?

I stood there, dazed. Dad came up. "What are you doing?" he asked. "Have you done any of your stretches?"

I shook my head slowly. What had just happened?

"Well, let's get on it. Things are about to start."

I searched the bleachers. "Is Grandpa Ed here yet?"

"He just came in."

I spotted Grandpa Ed making his way to where Mom, Gladys, and now Morgan sat. He saw me and gave me a thumbs-up. I waved back.

Dad and I started my warm-up. First, Dad called out stretches, and then different kicks, punches, and blocks. I followed, even though only half of me was listening. The other half jumped with the Jitters as big questions poured in. Questions like, what did a kiss on the cheek mean? Was it only to wish me luck, or did it mean something more?

"Spinning kick," Dad said.

I spun backward and my leg shot out behind me, right into Dad's hand. *Bam!*

"Watch the contact, Brendan," Dad warned. "Forward jump kick."

I jumped up and extended my leg from my knee. This time Dad pushed back when my foot hit his palm. I lost my balance and fell on my butt. My face burned hot.

"What's going on?"

I got up slowly.

"Are you *trying* to make contact?"

I didn't know whether I was actually trying or just not concentrating hard enough. But I for sure wanted him to know I wasn't weak. And I wasn't a geek. Or an egghead. I shrugged, then quickly added, "No, sir," when Dad's eyebrows lifted. We did a few more moves. I was careful not to make contact.

Dad put his hand on my shoulder. "Look, I realize I've been on you a lot recently—but you've worked hard and you'll do well."

Dad always gave me a pep talk before a competition. Usually I gobbled up his words as if they were candy. They gave me a last shot of energy before going into the ring. But this time his words just sat on my shoulder, as heavy as his hand pressing down on me.

"You're going to tell the referee you just tested for brown stripe, right?"

If I told the ref I'd only recently been promoted, he'd probably give me a break and I wouldn't have to do the form for brown stripes, *Hwa-Rang*, which I hadn't had time to learn yet. Instead I could do the form for purple belts, *Toi-Gye*, which I knew backwards and forwards after the last two weeks of practicing.

I nodded.

"Good." Dad knocked me in the arm with his fist. "Go get 'em, partner."

I joined Khal at the edge of our ring, where he sat watching the junior blue belts perform their *hyungs*. We'd be next. "Hey," I said.

"Hey." Khal bumped into me. "How's your girlfriend?"

"For the last time, she's *not* my girlfriend."

"Oh yeah?" He grinned. "Then why'd she kiss you over there under the basketball hoop?"

The hairs on my arms stood on end. "I don't know. I mean, she didn't. She was just wishing me good luck."

"Come on. Just admit it. You like her."

"No I don't."

"Then why do you act so funny around her?"

"I *don't*." I got hot again. I had heated up and cooled down so many times since getting there, I was like one giant weather system.

"You get all serious and scientific whenever she's around."

"That's the way I am!"

"You like her."

"Say it again and you'll be sorry."

Khal shrugged. "You like her."

I gritted my teeth and narrowed my eyes. I jumped up and was about to walk away when the judge called for the purple belts. We lined up and he reminded us of the rules. We'd execute our form one at a time. At the end, if two or more were tied, each one would perform the *hyung* once more so the judges could select a winner.

I was up first, which often happened with a last name that started near the beginning of the alphabet. I bowed to the referee, then approached him to make my request to do *Toi-Gye*. He agreed.

"*Kam sa ham nida, nim,*" I said, then bowed again and entered the ring, making sure not to look at the bleachers—where Morgan sat cheering in her head and where Gladys was for sure waving that foam finger. The judge gave me the okay to start.

I nailed each movement, never once losing focus. Double-fisted punch. Forward kick. Right punch. Left punch. Dad had made me do this *hyung* so many times I could have done it in my sleep. In fact, I probably had. My favorite part was a series of crescent kicks. A crescent is a spinning high kick to the side that ends with a stomp to represent crushing your enemy's ankle. Stomp. Stomp . . .

Stomp. Stomp. I did a one-eighty with each kick, my arms up and out to the sides like Godzilla marching through town.

I finished the form without a hitch. "Ha!" I bowed and kneeled with my back to the judges as they tallied my score.

Gladys hollered. "Woo-hoo!" I looked over to see the finger flying high. Grandpa Ed had his thumb and first finger in his mouth. He let out a shrill whistle.

After another boy and then a girl, it was Khal's turn. He entered the ring, bowed, and waited. Wasn't he going to ask permission to do *Toi-Gye*, too?

"*Shi jak*," the ref said, signaling for Khal to begin. I shrank inside. Khal had come in prepared to do *Hwa-Rang*. How had he gotten it down so quickly? He must have practiced 24/7 since our promotion test. His moves were as sharp as a samurai sword. I didn't like being jealous of my best friend, but he was making me look bad.

"Hee-*yah*!" Khal shouted, finishing the form. More hollering and finger waving from Gladys.

A few more kids performed. The three judges huddled to compare our scores. The head judge faced us and called out two names: Khalfani's and mine. *Shoot*. I would rather have had Khal win it outright than have to compete in a tiebreaker.

I went first again, but this time, right in the middle of the jump in which I'm supposed to land in a cross stance—right foot over left—I glanced at the risers.

Big mistake. Morgan stared intensely, watching my every move.

I lost my balance and stumbled. I recovered the best I could—being sure to make the last few punches strong and convincing—then kneeled, breathing hard. I kept my eyes on my hands, clenched in my lap. *Dumb, dumb, dumb*. Had Khal seen me look at Morgan? Had *Dad*?

When it was his turn, Khal punched and kicked, no fumbles or missteps. His eyes stayed glued to one spot the whole time, as if he were taking on one of the kick-boxers from his Jujitsu Rumble video game.

He was named the winner.

I was fine with him winning—honestly, it didn't mean that much to me—but still, I was mad at myself for making such a dumb mistake. I'd have to figure out something to tell Dad when he asked why I'd lost focus.

Khal and I bowed to each other, then headed for the *kyepka* area. Of course he gave me a bad time about tripping myself, but at least he didn't say anything about Morgan.

After breaking boards, I went to sit with my family until time for sparring.

"You were fantastic, Boo," Mom said. She pulled my head down to kiss my forehead.

"Mo-om," I whispered. Didn't she know she shouldn't be kissing on me in front of all these people? Anywhere, really, but *especially* at a Tae Kwon Do tournament.

I avoided looking at Dad . . . and Morgan, who still sat next to Gladys.

"Save some sugar for me!" Gladys puckered her lips and swatted me with the floppy finger. I scooted past Mom and bent over for Gladys's kiss. No use trying to deny Gladys.

Grandpa Ed reached over Gladys and slapped me on the back. "Way to go, kiddo. You looked great out there. That board-breaking stuff is dynamite!"

I smiled, finally. My grandpa had been there to see me.

Morgan slid over, making space for me between her and Gladys. "You were awesome!" she whispered in my ear. Her hand brushed mine.

A tingle ran from the ends of my fingers up my arm and down my back. All the way to my toes. And it wasn't the kind of tingle I got when I had a question. I had never felt a tingle like this.

"What happened on your *hyung*?" At the sound of Dad's voice the tingle turned into a prickling heat in my armpits.

Mom gave Dad a look, but he kept his eyes on me.

"I just lost focus for a second."

"There's no 'just' about it. You lost focus. How many times do I have to tell you, Brendan? When I was on patrol, a second could mean the difference between living and dying. You can't 'just' lose focus."

"Aren't you taking this a little seriously?" Grandpa Ed asked. "It's a sport. Not life or death."

"I second that!" Gladys said. "Leave the boy alone, Sam. The seniors rule on this one."

Dad's jaw clenched. He looked back out onto the floor.

I pulled my arms and legs in, trying not to touch Morgan and hoping she hadn't figured out that she had been the distraction.

When it was time to check in for the sparring competition, Dad walked with me to the sidelines. I'd seen Mom talking to him after the tense moment we'd had in the stands. "Look, this should be fun for you, but it's not only about fun. Do you understand what I'm saying?" he said.

Dad had told Mom boys like me got beat down. I would show him. I could be tough. I *was* tough.

I sat on the opposite side of the ring from Khal to watch the first two competitors spar. I didn't need him distracting me right now or accusing me of liking Morgan again—not that it would be a crime if I did. Jeez.

The four judges stood one to a corner, their flags ready. Each judge had two flags on wooden dowels, one red and one blue, which corresponded to the two contestants. The red contestant wore a red ribbon tied to the back of his belt. When one person kicked or punched in their opponent's "strike zone," the judges would raise that contestant's flag. If three out of four judges raised their flag, the striker got a point—half a point for a kick or punch made from the ground and a full point for a jumping one.

The first two contestants—two boys who looked at least fourteen, the upper end of the juniors division—were done quickly. The tall, skinny one who never stopped moving scored the three points needed to win in about a minute.

Next, the head referee called Khal and me. I was a little surprised Master Rickman had put us together in the first round. One of us would be going out.

We stood in the center of the ring. The referee tied the red ribbon to Khal's belt. Khal hopped from foot to foot while the ref reminded us of the rules. The strike zone—where we aimed for but couldn't actually touch—was anything waist up in the front, including the head and neck, and a six-inch strip down the spine in the back—no kidneys or shoulder blades. We were not to make contact with any part of the body, and if someone called for a time-out, the other contestant was to turn and kneel until the ref said to resume.

"You ready for the Brown-Stripe Bomber?" Khal whispered, still hopping around. He shook out his arms.

I narrowed my eyes. "Bring it on." Were we fooling around? Or had I just challenged my best friend to an actual fight?

"*Kyung ret,*" the referee said, reminding us to bow.

We bowed to him and then to each other. *"Choon bee."* Ready. *"Shi jak!"*

I went straight for Khal's middle with a standing side kick, figuring he was so busy dancing around he wouldn't be expecting it. Three judges raised flags. Half point to the Science Nerd.

I heard Dad on the sidelines. "That's right, Bren. Way to get in there!"

Khal jumped and kicked, but I blocked with my knee. I moved around him, jabbing, but he moved too fast for me to find an opening.

He jerked one way and I followed. As I moved, I lowered my guard and he punched at my chest. All four red flags flew up. Half point, Brown-Stripe Bomber.

"Good job, Khal!" his dad yelled. "Keep it up!"

Khal motioned as if to punch up high. My arms flew up and before I could recover, his foot shot toward my middle. He had been midflight, giving him another whole point.

Now it was my turn to dance. He wouldn't catch me standing still for even one millisecond. We moved around each other like binary stars, jabbing and kicking without extending our arms or legs very far. Neither of us wanted to give the other a chance to find a hole.

Dad shouted, "Time, Brendan! Time!"—telling me that our two minutes was almost up and if I didn't score a full point soon, Khal would be declared the winner.

"Strike, Brendan!" Dad yelled again.

"Hold steady, Khalfani!" Mr. Jones responded.

Show Dad what you can do.

Morgan is watching.

This is your chance.

My thoughts whirled. I jumped, spun, and extended my leg behind me—*pow!*—just as Khal rushed in for a punch.

I had jumped higher than I knew I could. My heel crashed into his face. *Crunch.*

Khal collapsed. "Aaah!" He covered his nose and mouth with both hands and curled in on himself. Blood poured down his arms. It was all over the front of his *do bok* and on the gym floor. And it didn't seem to be slowing down.

I reached out to help him up. He jerked away, moaning.

"Oh, man, I'm sorry, Khal. I'm sorry. I didn't mean to. It'll be all right."

The head referee nudged me out of the way. He and Khal's dad lifted Khal and walked him to an empty chair at the judges' table.

Everything in the gym had stopped. The bleachers were silent. All eyes were on the main ring.

I stood frozen, staring at the bright red puddle at my feet. A corner judge came over with a towel. "I'll do it," I said and kneeled to wipe up my friend's blood.

I kept my distance while they worked on getting Khal's nose to stop bleeding. Khal swiped at his eyes, but it was obvious he was crying.

Dad said something to Mr. Jones, then motioned for me to come over. Was he angry? What would he say? No doubt Mr. Jones was mad at me. And Khalfani, too.

What had happened? Why hadn't I pulled back?

"His nose is probably broken." Dad peered at me, his eyes two slits. "What were you thinking? *Were* you thinking?"

I couldn't even begin to tell Dad all that was going on in my head when I'd delivered that kick.

"We'll talk about this later," Dad said gruffly. "His dad's taking him to the ER."

"Can I go with them?" I asked.

Dad shook his head. "You need to stay here. Support the others from your *dojang*."

"But I want to go!" My chest throbbed as if I'd been the one who'd gotten kicked. The stinging behind my eyes came up on me so fast I didn't have time to blink the water away. I turned my back to make sure no one saw. "It was an accident," I mumbled. My plan had been to prove I was tough, and here I was, crying like a complete chump.

The head judge called Dad over. Mom came up and put her arm around me. "You okay?"

I planted my face in her shoulder. I didn't care if it wasn't the brown-stripe-warrior thing to do.

When I looked up, Khal and his dad were walking toward the exit.

Dad came back to where Mom and I stood. "The ref says technically Khal forfeits. You advance to the next round, but with a strong warning."

Mom's forehead crinkled. "Sam, I don't—"

"It's Brendan's decision." Dad waited for my response.

"I don't want to."

Dad's face was still as stone. He walked over to the head ref to tell him I was done.

I strode past the bleachers and headed outside. Morgan called my name, but I kept on walking. I pushed through the front doors of the Y into the bright, cool air. Khal's dad and stepmom helped him into the front of their silver Mercedes. Dori climbed into the back. When she saw me out the rear window, she stuck out her tongue.

I blinked and squinted against the sunlight, harsh even with the solid cloud cover, and stood there shivering, long after they had driven away.

CHAPTER 21

I called Khal first thing Sunday morning to see how he was, but his stepmom said he didn't feel like coming to the phone. I told her six times how sorry I was. "Will you tell him?" I asked. "That I'm sorry."

"He should probably hear that from you, don't you think?" Mrs. Jones said. Her voice snipped like the lab scissors we'd been using in Mr. H's class to dissect sheep eyes. "You'll see him on Monday."

My family had gone to Shari's after the tournament as planned, but as far as I was concerned there wasn't much to celebrate. I'd laughed a little when Gladys told Grandpa Ed about the time she got invited onto the stage at a Tina Turner tribute concert, but other than that I'd stayed quiet.

Mom must have been able to tell I was still worked up about the whole thing. She came into my room

Sunday night and asked if I'd gotten to talk to Khal. When I said no, she told me not to worry, that it would get worked out eventually. I said, "I know," but I wasn't sure how, especially if my best friend wouldn't talk to me.

Khal showed up to school the next day with a huge bandage sort of like an X over his nose. His puffy eyelids made him look sleepy and he had dark bruises under both eyes.

I started to walk up to him to ask how he was doing, but he just glared and stepped around me. I glanced at the kids goofing off at their lockers, bit the side of my cheek, and kept on going.

After homeroom, a group huddled around Khal, wanting to know what had happened. The rest of the week, everywhere I went I heard kids calling out things like "There goes Jackie Chan!" and "Don't hurt me, Jackie!" Someone must have told an older brother or sister, because even some of the seventh and eighth graders started calling me Jackie when they saw me coming into school.

The one person who wasn't saying anything to me was Khalfani, my *former* best friend.

Morgan was encouraging. "It's not like you meant to do it," she said on our way to Mr. Hammond's class.

I glanced at her out of the corner of my eye.

"*Did* you?" We stopped outside the room.

"No!" I bit the side of my cheek again. A bump had formed where I'd been chewing on it all morning.

"I'm sorry. I knew that." She looked at me sheepishly. "He's still your best friend, isn't he?"

I felt my forehead wrinkle even as I nodded. "Yeah, I guess." It was time to change the subject. "Our report is due next Monday. Do you want to come over this Saturday to finish it? You could stay for dinner." I had already checked with Mom.

Morgan practically vibrated—I guessed from excitement—like a quartz crystal in a watch. "Definitely! I'm sure my parents will say yes." The bell rang and we hurried to our seats.

Whoa, I thought, realizing what I had just done. Gladys could never find out.

Log Entry—Thursday, November 1

Went trick-or-treating with Oscar and Marcus last night. I was Albert Einstein. Oscar was a magician. Marcus was a football player. Mom frizzed out my hair and put in flour to turn it white. I wore a bushy mustache, a lab coat, and goggles, and carried around a smoking beaker full of dry ice. It was my best costume yet.

Didn't see Khal. We've trick-or-treated together for the last two years, ever since meeting at Tae Kwon Do, but we didn't even talk about it this time. Technically, we haven't talked about anything since I broke his nose. I overheard him bragging to Cordé that he and Dwight David trick-or-treated at the army base, dressed like commandos with camouflage paint on their faces.

Are Khal and I still best friends? The last few days it's seemed more like we're enemies. Like we're the ones at war.

CHAPTER 22

Saturday, I stood in front of my bathroom mirror trying to get my hair to lie down. Maybe Dad's pomade would help. I snuck into Mom and Dad's bathroom. I couldn't find the pomade, but I found Dad's bottle of cologne.

Excalibur?

Dad was in the living room watching a football game. Mom was busy in the kitchen. I unscrewed the cap on the dark brown bottle and took a whiff. Not bad. I double-checked to make sure no one was around, then splashed a little in my palms and slapped my face, like I'd seen Dad do. I sniffed my pits. Better to be safe than sorry. I dabbed some under each arm.

I went to my room to see what my lizard was up to. He was totally chill. Just hanging out on his vine. I wished I could be that relaxed, but my insides were jumping around like the contestants on this dance show Khal and I used to watch on BET . . . back when we were friends. "Turn on the charm for me tonight, okay, Einstein? Let her hold you without turning brown. Impress her with your dewlap. You know, that kind of stuff." Einstein stared off into the distance, not paying any attention to me at all.

When the doorbell rang, I took my time. I didn't want to look too much in a rush. I took the stairs slowly, ran my hand over my hair one more time, and pulled open the door.

Morgan waved to her dad, who waved back and then drove away. "Hi," she said. She smiled.

"Hi." Something was different.

"Umm . . . were you planning to let me in? It's kind of cold out here. Not to mention it's raining."

"Oh. Right." I stepped back and she came inside, toting her backpack. "Where are your braces?" I asked, finally realizing why she looked different.

"Gone!" Morgan beamed, except now the only thing that sparkled were her white teeth. "I've been counting the days for the last two months—basically since school started."

Dad yelled from the living room. "Brendan, shut the door! We're getting a draft up here."

I shut the door while Morgan took off her shoes. Her teeth looked . . . nice. But I didn't say so because compliments can be tricky. I'd learned that from listening to Dad compliment Mom.

If I said I liked the change, then she might think I didn't like the way her teeth looked before, but honestly, I'd never thought at all about her teeth—only her glittery braces. But now that I could see her teeth, I thought they were nice—straight and perfectly spaced, not too big or too small, like polished pieces of squared-off chalcedony.

She sniffed the air. "What's that smell?"

"My mom's making pizza."

Her nose wrinkled and she shook her head. "It's spicy, but not like pepperoni. More like perfume."

Uh-oh. The cologne. I jammed my elbows into my sides and shrugged as best I could with my arms glued to my body.

"It's not a bad smell. . . ."

I turned with stiff arms and took the stairs two at a time, trying to get away from Morgan's nose.

"Hi, Morgan," Mom called.

Morgan followed me into the kitchen. She waved at Dad as we went by. "Hello, Mr. Buckley," she said.

"How are you?" he asked.

"Fine, thank you. Hi, Mrs. Buckley."

Mom held out a platter of veggies with hummus dip. "I made a snack to hold you over until dinner."

Morgan took a celery stick. I passed. I just wanted

to get to work on our report—and get away from my parents.

Morgan crunched her celery, then ran her tongue over her teeth. "Wow! Nothing for the strings to get stuck in. It feels so weird!" She leaned against the counter as if she planned to stay for a while.

Mom pushed the dough this way and that on the pizza pan. "So, how are things going for you at Eastmont? Do you miss being homeschooled?" Mom asked.

"Not really . . . although I guess being in public school is kind of hard sometimes."

Morgan thought something about school was hard? I had just been about to go scrub off the cologne, but now I was curious to hear what else Morgan would say.

"How so?" Mom asked.

"Don't tell my parents this . . . I don't want them to have any reason to pull me out, because I want to be there, I really do . . . but sometimes—maybe a lot of the time—I don't feel like I fit in."

"That *is* hard. Why don't you feel like you fit in?"

"I'm a geek!"

At least she knew it.

Mom laughed. "I don't know about—"

"No, I am. And it doesn't even really bother me."

Wow—she didn't *mind* being a geek?

"When kids start talking about popular bands or songs or TV shows, I have no idea what they're talking about. Sometimes I laugh and nod as if I do, but I don't, and I don't like being fake like that."

"Have you made many friends? Surely there must be some other girls who don't care whether you know about that stuff."

"Honestly?" Morgan paused. She stared at the back of Mom's head. "Brendan is my best friend."

What? Had she just said what I thought she'd said? I gulped. Blood pulsed in my ears.

"Oh?" Mom was trying to sound casual, I could tell. "Well, he *is* a great kid." Mom looked over her shoulder and smiled.

I rolled my eyes. Morgan's face had gone all gooey, like one of Grandpa Ed's maple donuts. I got seriously interested in the hummus and carrot sticks.

"How does your mom like her new job?" Mom asked.

I interrupted. "We should probably get to work."

Morgan acted as if she hadn't even heard me. "She loves it. She's taking me out on her research vessel the first weekend in December. I am *so* excited!"

"That sounds like fun," Mom said.

Geesh. Had Morgan come over to finish our report or to talk to my mom? "Hey, do you want to see Einstein?" Maybe *I* couldn't get Morgan's attention, but my anole surely would.

"Actually, I was wondering if you'd let Brendan come with us." Morgan looked at me. "I mean, if you want to."

My stomach flipped.

Morgan's gaze returned to Mom, which was a good thing because I was about to pass out. Morgan wanted me to stay with her, on a boat, *for a whole weekend*? And I'd thought pizza with my family on a Saturday night was a big deal!

"Go with you?" Mom asked.

Morgan nodded. "Yes. On the boat."

Mom glanced to where I stood stiffly in the doorway. "That sounds like a pretty big imposition on your mom while she's trying to do her job."

"She already said it was okay. Believe me, she'll put us to work. 'Academic enrichment,' she calls it. She loves teaching. She taught science for our homeschool group—that was seven kids. Two of us will be a piece of cake."

"Is that something you'd like to do, Bren?" Mom looked at me again.

Uhh, yeah! I pulled my lips down, shrugged, and nodded, playing it cool.

"Mom loves what we've been doing with our science project. She thinks Brendan is brilliant." Morgan glanced my way, then looked at her hands.

I buzzed from head to toe. I crossed my arms tightly and tried not to let the chain reaction that had been set off in my body show.

"Well, I'll talk to Brendan's dad, and I'd like to talk to your mom about it, too."

"No problem!" Morgan flashed her big smile again.

Her *nice*, big smile. She turned to me. "Ready to finish our report?"

I was and I wasn't. The whole time we sat in front of my computer (after I'd ducked into the bathroom to scrub off the cologne), all I could think about was me and Morgan on a boat, being scientists, together.

CHAPTER 23

On Monday, Mr. Hammond had reserved the computer lab during third period for our science class. We spent the hour filling out the online application, attaching our various photo and video files, and submitting our projects for consideration for the grand prize of five thousand dollars.

"We should know who the finalists are by early next month," Mr. H told the class.

I was confident Morgan's and my entry could win something, in spite of the big poo-poo-palooza in my basement. We had submitted a really good report based on our findings, with lots of practical ideas for methane collection and recycling that would definitely make the world a better place. That could *save* the world, really. I just hoped the judges would agree.

Waiting to find out about the contest is torture! Also counting the days until I get to go out on the research vessel with Morgan and Dr. Belcher. It's going to be awesome!

I hold Einstein every once in a while now. He doesn't turn brown. I think he actually kind of likes it. The other day, he climbed onto my hand all by himself. Today, I caught a spider in Mom and Dad's bedroom and fed it to him. I figured it could be sort of like his turkey, since it's Thanksgiving and all. It was gone in about three seconds flat. Mom was happy to know he eats spiders and said Einstein can help himself any time. I'll probably give him one every now and then as a special treat. Spiders are a lot easier to catch than Einstein was!

Khal and I are still not talking much. More and more it's him, Dwight David, and Cordé sitting together at lunch and Oscar, Marcus, and me sitting somewhere else. Sometimes Morgan joins us. Marcus and Oscar seem cool with it.

Finally, the big weekend for the marine expedition arrived, except I would only be on the boat for the day. Dad didn't want me sleeping over with a girl.

I'd wanted to tell him it was a *research vessel*, not

some romantic cruise, but I kept my mouth shut. One day was better than nothing. Morgan's mom was willing to come back in just to drop me off at the pier, which made me feel sort of embarrassed, but I wasn't about to turn down the offer.

In the car on our way to the marina, Dad asked how school was going.

"Good," I said.

"Older kids giving you any problems?"

"Nah," I said. We passed the Tae Kwon Do studio.

Dad spoke again. "Everything all right with Khalfani?"

I felt as if I'd been injected with cola. I fizzed from head to toe. *Not really*, I thought.

Khal's nose was back to normal, but our friendship sure wasn't. I'd tried to apologize to his face a couple of times. The second time, he just said, "Forget it, man," but if he really meant it, then why didn't he ever want to be my sparring partner at Tae Kwon Do anymore? Why hadn't we gone trick-or-treating together? And why, when he'd shot off his launcher with Dwight David, had he invited Oscar and Marcus but not me?

I had no idea how to make things right with Khal, and even less of an idea how to talk about it with my dad, so I just said, "Yeah," and nodded my head. "Everything's fine."

We pulled up at a stoplight. "He hasn't been around much lately."

"Neither have you." I hadn't meant it to come out so strong. I sat stiffly, worried I'd crossed the line into back-talk territory.

The car rolled forward again. Dad kept his eyes straight ahead. "I've been tied up, I know. But I'll get a break over Christmas. We'll spend more time together then. All right?"

I looked at him out of the corner of my eye and nodded, but I wanted to say I wished he'd never gone back to school. I wanted to say I wasn't sure if I wanted to keep going in Tae Kwon Do.

I *wanted* to ask why he had never shown any interest in our methane experiment or the science competition.

But I didn't.

Dad and I walked the pier at Dock Street Marina. Even if somehow I couldn't find a sixty-five-foot research vessel named *Olympus*, I knew I'd be able to spot Morgan's huge smile a hundred yards away.

I was buzzing with excitement—mostly about getting on the boat, but honestly, a lot of me was looking forward to spending the day with Morgan. This time I'd skipped the cologne, though.

My duffel bag bumped against my hip. I had packed my Tacoma Rainiers cap, a sack lunch, sunglasses, and an extra pair of shoes, which Mom had made me bring in case my sneakers got wet. And, of course, I had brought my logbook. I knew a lot of kids kept their writing on their computers, in digital diaries and online folders. But a real notebook, made of real paper—that was the way for me, just like scientists had been doing for decades. Plus, I couldn't exactly have lugged my desktop PC onto the *Olympus.*

"Be sure to do everything you're asked," Dad said.

"Okay."

"Show respect."

I nodded. We walked in silence for several paces.

"So, you like this girl?"

"*Morgan?*"

"Mm-hmm. Do you like her?"

I swallowed. It felt as if a test tube were going down my throat sideways. My palm felt moist against the strap of my bag.

"I'll take that as a yes."

We kept our faces forward, still walking.

"I—I like her okay."

Dad's eyebrow rose. A couple of nights ago, he'd come into my room and handed me a book called *What's Going On Down There?* It wasn't hard to figure out what it was about.

Sitting there, staring at the book, I'd felt as though I'd shrunk to the size of my green anole, and a basking lamp with too much wattage was cooking me.

"Let me know if you have any questions," Dad had said before heading out the door.

I'd read the thing cover to cover and I had *plenty* of questions, but I'd chosen just to write them in my logbook. I could seek out answers later.

My eyes scanned the marina. I was about to say there was nothing to worry about—Morgan and I were just science partners—when I spotted the boat moored at the end of a dock. Morgan jumped onto the pier from the boat's deck. "Hi, Brendan! Hi, Mr. Buckley!"

Dr. Belcher followed close behind. She and Dad shook hands. "I don't think we've ever officially met. I'm Meg Belcher, Morgan's mom." I was surprised by how pretty she was. Taller than my mom, for sure, because she was taller than me, with long, wavy brown hair pulled back in a ponytail, and wide-set brown eyes—exactly like Morgan's.

"Sam Buckley. Glad to meet you."

"You as well. Ready to join our crew, Brendan?"

"Aye, aye, Captain!"

"Oh, no." Dr. Belcher shook her hands in front of her. "That would be that man over there. Captain Dennis!"

An older man wearing a fisherman's hat and spraying a hose on deck waved.

"I presume you're outfitted with life preservers and rafts," Dad said.

"Survival suits . . . the whole nine yards," Dr. Belcher replied. "We'll do a safety demo for Brendan before we take off. And we've got two radios—one dedicated to channel sixteen for emergencies. The Coast Guard is just a call away. Your department has a boat, too, doesn't it?"

"We do."

"I thought I'd seen a Tacoma PD boat trolling the bay. Be assured, our captain has been piloting this vessel for thirty years—first as a commercial fisherman and now for us. He's a pro." Dr. Belcher looked up at the cloudless sky. "I think this past week's rain went away just for us. So, what do you say we get to it?" She climbed on board. "We'll have Brendan back around four this afternoon. Sound good?"

"That's fine." Dad raised his eyebrows at me. "You good?"

I nodded. I was *more* than good.

He slapped me on the back and I followed Morgan onto the boat.

A two-story enclosure sat at the bow of the boat. The only way to the second level appeared to be metal rungs, which led to the door of what I guessed was the cockpit, or whatever it was called on a boat. I'd have to find out. Captain Dennis had disappeared into there a minute ago.

Another ladder, directly across from where I stood, led to an upper deck—a narrow strip outfitted with a bench. Below that, on the main deck, was a sink area with a long metal countertop.

The deck was mostly a wide-open space, but with lots of stuff—I presumed research stuff—sitting around.

Hoses and tethered ropes hung everywhere. Large metal hatches made me wonder what was down below. Three large spools of different types of cable lay anchored on their sides, and there was something that looked like a Mars rover but with jets instead of wheels. "That's the ROV," Morgan said. "Remotely operated vehicle. Suzanne is awesome at maneuvering it."

A stocky, middle-aged woman wearing rubber overalls and boots appeared in the doorway of the enclosure's lower level. Her cheeks looked sunburned. "I'm pretty darn good at Super Mario World, too." She went to the side of the boat and pulled in the ropes keeping us tied to the dock.

During the orientation and safety demonstration, I learned that the left side of the boat as you face the front is the port side; the right side is called starboard. Kevin, the grad assistant doing the demo, told me the names came from early European explorers who sailed their ships around the coast of Africa. The left of the boat was the side closest to the ports as they traveled, and the right was the side from which they navigated by the stars. I would definitely record that in my logbook later.

"Can you swim?" Kevin asked. He picked up an orange life jacket from the deck.

"I'm all right, I guess."

Suzanne stopped and stared. "Just all right? Stop the boat!" she called out.

I froze.

Captain Dennis turned and looked from where he stood steering the boat.

Morgan whispered in my ear. "She's only kidding."

"Sorry, Dennis!" Suzanne called again. "Just razzing our initiate!" She and Kevin exchanged smiles.

I took a deep breath and tried to smile, as well, but I was still a little shaken up.

"You won't fall in." Suzanne fiddled with a circular contraption made out of ten pieces of PVC pipe standing on end. "But if you do, Kevin will jump in to save you."

"Actually, I'll use my orca call to get a whale to do it," Kevin said. "Don't you think that would make for a better story back at school?"

I smiled for real this time. "That would be cool."

"Seriously," Morgan said. "If that happens, I'll have to fall in, too."

Kevin said we didn't need to wear the life jackets unless it got really rocky, which was unlikely given the clear skies. "Just don't go trying to walk the railings, and everything should be copacetic."

After that, we toured the boat, starting with the "dry lab"—a bay filled with monitors and a couple of laptops right off the galley, which included a small kitchen and table with stools bolted to the ground. The bathroom (called the head for some reason—I was too embarrassed to ask why in front of Morgan) was smaller than a closet, and the bunk area was not much bigger.

Seeing the close quarters, I was glad I wouldn't be

spending the night. Turned out men and women bunked in the same small space. Only a sheet of plywood and twelve inches of air would have separated Morgan and me while we slept. *Way* too close for comfort. You couldn't even *whisper* in your sleep without having the whole crew hear you. Never mind something more embarrassing.

Finally, it was time to get to work. Captain Dennis slowed the boat to the point where I couldn't even tell we were still moving. Dr. Belcher showed us how to lower the PVC contraption—a rosette, she called it—into the water until it was at just the right depth. The pipes were fitted with lids that were open when we lowered the rosette, but with a push of a button, they snapped shut, trapping water inside to be analyzed later.

The really cool thing, though, was the instrument in the center of the rosette, called the CTD because it measured the water's conductivity (or salinity), temperature, and depth. Other sensors on the rosette could detect oxygen concentration, light levels, even fluorescence. All this live data was sent to the computers in the dry lab. Dr. Belcher said we were basically tracking the weather of the ocean.

"A lot of what I do is water sampling," she said as we waited for the cable to bring the CTD back up to the surface. Morgan and I helped haul the rosette over the railing, then watched as Dr. Belcher and Kevin transferred the water samples into bottles. Morgan and I recorded the bottle numbers into a logbook and then put them in a cooler that would keep them the right temperature until they could be unloaded at the onshore lab.

"I want people to understand the impact we make," Dr. Belcher said, handing me another sample bottle. "Like right now, it's right after Thanksgiving, so we're probably going to detect spices—lots of nutmeg and cinnamon."

"Cinnamon?" I said. "In the water?" I held up the bottle and looked at its murky contents. Looking at the water reminded me of an experiment I'd once done to observe how sediments form layers at the bottom of a lake or ocean.

"Yep. Whatever we put down the sink ends up out here. And that affects the creatures who live here."

The other big thing Dr. Belcher did was study phytoplankton. Certain phytoplankton sometimes produce neurotoxins that build up in the shellfish that eat them. The neurotoxins can kill people who eat the shellfish. PSP, she called it: paralytic shellfish poisoning.

"So if you're having shrimp and your lips start to tingle," Kevin said, "stop eating. Unless it's just the Cajun seasoning."

How would you know the difference? I thought. I made a note in my log. "Tingling lips = stop eating!"

Over the next few hours, we took four more samples in very spread-out locations. Then it was time for a quick lunch break on deck. On the sixth drop of the CTD,

Morgan and I went to the dry lab to watch the live data coming in. Suzanne explained what all the numbers and squiggly lines on the screen meant.

I was having a great time, but after a while, I started getting a little restless. The numbers and squiggles were all running together. While Morgan was engrossed in hearing Suzanne's answer to her latest question, I slipped outside. I climbed the ladder to the second level and looked out. Islands rose from the water to the west. It smelled like ocean—fishy, metallic, dense—lots of negatively charged ions hanging around. I took a deep breath. Ahhh . . . this was the life.

"Isn't it gorgeous?" Morgan came up and stood by my side. "I'd love to live on one of those islands someday."

I'd seen only a handful of houses on any of the land we'd passed. "Wouldn't you feel kind of . . . cut off?"

"I like being by myself." She gazed into my eyes. "Or maybe with one other person."

Between the icy blast of wind and my heart fibrillating, I practically choked on my own breath. My legs started to shake. I clutched the cold railing and looked away.

I was about to say I needed to visit the head when Kevin came on deck. "Hey!" he called up. "We're going back to shore. You guys wanna play cards?"

"Sure!" Morgan moved toward the ladder.

Whew! Saved by a card game. I took one last glance at the dark, mysterious waters, then followed Morgan down the ladder. My heart still beat hard and my legs felt wobbly, but I made it inside.

Kevin and I sat on one side of the table in the galley. Morgan and Suzanne sat on the other. Kevin told us the rules for rummy as he passed out the cards.

A half hour later, the girls were beating us bad. Kevin was tallying up the score after a hand when Morgan's mom came into the room carrying her laptop.

"Morgan, I got an email from Dad I think you'll want to see. Brendan, too." She set the computer in front of Morgan. I came around and stood near her—not too close, just close enough to see the screen. What would Morgan's dad have sent that would involve me?

"What is it?" Morgan looked up at her mom. She grabbed my wrist and guided me to the stool beside her. Suzanne had gotten up for a coffee refill.

"Just read." Dr. Belcher crossed her arms and smiled. Suzanne peered over Morgan's shoulder.

I quickly scanned the email. "Mr. Hammond called the house . . . the kids' project . . . only sixth graders from Washington . . . regional FINALISTS!!!"

My eyes stayed glued to the word *finalists*. My whole body felt spring-loaded, as if I might shoot from the table and ricochet around the room. If I hadn't been in front of a bunch of people I didn't really know, I would have jumped up and down and yelled at the top of my lungs. We'd done it!

Morgan threw her arms around me and squeezed so

hard she almost knocked the air out of me. My head bobbled as she bounced.

"*Eeeeeeee!*" Her screech sent a shooting pain through my head. I would have covered my ears, but my arms were locked to my sides. "Can you believe it? Can you believe it?" She jiggled some more, but she still didn't let go. "We're finalists in a *national science competition!*"

I pulled away to get some distance between her mouth and my eardrum. Finally, she jumped up and transferred her vise grip to her mom.

Kevin reached across the table and slapped my shoulder. "Congratulations! That's quite the accomplishment."

I kept reading the email. "Your dad says the national winner will be announced in a couple of weeks."

"Mom, can you believe it? I feel like a real scientist!"

Morgan's mom put her hand on the side of Morgan's face. "You've *been* a real scientist since the days when you sat in your high chair throwing things to the ground to hear what kind of sounds they would make."

Something about the way Morgan's mom looked into Morgan's eyes made my heart feel as though it were in one of those taffy-pulling machines. Dr. Belcher put her cheek against the top of Morgan's head. "I'm so proud of you, honey."

If only . . .

My Adam's apple suddenly felt about twice its normal size. I sucked up the snot that had started to flow and gulped hard. I wasn't about to *cry* again, was I? What was my problem lately?

Morgan's mom put her hand on my shoulder. "You too, Brendan. I'm very proud of both of you."

My eyes roamed the tiled floor. "Thanks." The word came out more garbled than I meant it to. My throat still felt kind of thick.

"We need to celebrate this," Suzanne said. "Root beer, anyone?" She went to the minifridge.

"Yes!" Morgan said. "Do you want one, Brendan?"

The taffy machine in my chest stopped pulling. I looked up. "Sure." I cleared my throat. "That's my favorite."

"I'll take one to Captain Dennis," Kevin said, "and tell him the good news." He winked as he took a bottle and climbed the ladder to the pilothouse.

We stayed at the table. Suzanne and Morgan's mom sat across from us. When Morgan's hand slipped into mine, I didn't pull away. I observed the warm softness of it. *Nice.*

Kevin returned and sat at the end of the table. He may have seen us holding hands because his lips turned up in a sort-of smile, but, thankfully, he didn't say anything.

I sipped my root beer, listening to the adults tell stories of times they'd been out on the *Olympus*—drifting through glowing algae, glimpsing the glistening moonlit bodies of killer whales, working hard to keep this watery home safe for its inhabitants. To me, these people were the superheroes.

The word *finalist* kept repeating in my head. I felt more excited than when Khal and I had made our first belt promotion in Tae Kwon Do, or even when Mom told me I was getting Einstein for my birthday.

And I kept my hand in Morgan's as long as I could— until the last story was told.

<u>Log Entry—Saturday, December 1</u>

Observation: The skin on the inside of a girl's hand is as soft and warm as freshly made cotton candy.

CHAPTER 24

On Sunday, Gladys and Grandpa Ed came for dinner, as usual. Mom made my favorite meal—fried shrimp and baked potatoes—to celebrate the finalist announcement.

I'd told Dad our good news as soon as I'd stepped off the *Olympus*. He'd seemed surprised and shown some enthusiasm, but he hadn't gotten nearly as excited as everyone on the boat—people I'd just met that day.

"To my grandson," Grandpa Ed said, raising his glass of sparkling cider, "a chip off the old rock!"

Gladys clinked her glass against mine. She narrowed her eyes and looked at me intently. "Your Grampa Clem would have been *busting* his buttons."

I took a quick gulp of cider to get the lump in my throat to go down. If only Grampa Clem *were* there with us. Maybe somehow he knew. . . .

I glanced at Dad. He frowned into his plate.

"Your dad and I are very proud of you, as well," Mom said, filling in the silence that had followed Gladys's words. "Whether you win or not, you've already achieved something huge. Right, Sam?"

Dad looked up. A fault line ran across his forehead. "What? Oh, right. Good work, Bren."

Why was it so hard for me to believe that he meant that?

———

The next day at school, Principal Salinas made an announcement during homeroom about Morgan and me being regional finalists. After homeroom, Khal came up to me at my desk. "Hey," he said.

"Hey," I said.

"Congratulations." He held out his hand.

I shook it.

"It's really cool that you and Morgan were chosen." A smile crept onto his face. "Even if your experiment *was* totally nasty."

I smiled in return. "Thanks." I looked at my desktop, then back up at Khal. "Are you still mad . . . about your nose?"

"Nah." He shook his head. "Thanks to you, I became a real chick magnet there for a few weeks." It was true. Girls had waited on him hand and foot while his nose had been broken. "I kept those bandages on a whole week longer than I needed to!" He laughed. It looked like Khal and I could get back to being friends again.

In science class, Mr. Hammond threw Morgan and me a pizza party. Everyone was really excited for us, even Aadesh. I'd thought he might have been a little sore over not getting chosen himself.

Dwight David hovered around Morgan like a bee near a flower. I'd been trying to be nicer to him since I'd found out about his dad being deployed overseas, but right then, he was really getting on my nerves. He kept asking Morgan if she wanted a refill on her pop and bringing her slices of pizza and saying what an awesome thing it was that *her* experiment had been picked.

Lauren Dweck handed me a folded piece of paper with a pencil drawing on the front. It said "Brendan the Super Scientist" across the top. In the picture, I stood at a counter wearing a lab coat and protective goggles. The beakers in my hands were bubbling and steaming. I opened the card. "Good luck in the national contest! I hope you win!!! ♥ xoxo ♥, Lauren."

"Thanks," I said. I glanced around, trying to figure out where to stash the card before one of the guys saw it.

"You're welcome." She stood there beaming.

"Um . . . it's a good drawing."

"Thanks," she said. "I really hope you win."

"Thanks." A seat was open at Cordé's table. Khal was over there, too. "Well . . . I'll see you later." I folded up the card and stuffed it in my back pocket, then grabbed another piece of pizza and went to join them.

The guys gave me a hard time about thinking I was too good for them now that I was a science contest winner, but I knew they were just playing. We joked and laughed. It felt good to be back to normal with Khal.

During lunch break, Khal wanted to play football since we'd already eaten in science. I told the guys I'd meet them on the field after I put some things in my locker, which I didn't mention included Lauren's card. When I was done, I headed outside.

"Brendan, over here!" Khal waved his arms in the air.

I jogged over, an occasional raindrop hitting my face. Khal turned just in time to catch Marcus's pass. He zigged and zagged while Oscar and Dwight David chased after him. Khal zipped past the tree that we used as a goal line, spiked the ball, and did his end zone dance—flapping knees, bobbing head, and disco finger up and down.

"Hi . . . Brendan," Oscar said, between gulps of air. His cheeks were pink and his hairline was sweaty, even though the air was nippy. Dwight David flopped to the ground with his arms and legs spread wide.

Marcus and Khal came over. Khal tossed me the ball. "Jaivier Brown and his boys challenged us to a game after school."

"Yeah," Dwight David said. "Five on five. We're going to get thrashed."

"Totally thrashed," Oscar said, still huffing. "They play on a club team. They're really good."

"I . . ." I started to say I couldn't be there after school. Morgan and I had agreed to go to her house to research a new experiment idea—this one on water pollution.

"Why are we standing around?" Marcus grabbed the ball from me. "Let's play."

Oh, well. I'd play with them now and convince Cordé to take my place after school. Or maybe I'd tell Morgan we could get together the next day. One thing I knew for sure: The guys couldn't find out about Morgan and me and the whole hand-holding thing. I was still feeling confused about what that had meant and what Morgan might be expecting next.

I got in a three-point stance across from Khal, who hiked the ball to Marcus, then took off running. I stayed on him like white on milk . . . until I saw Morgan. She crossed the field, headed straight toward us. It started to rain for real.

Suddenly, Dwight David, who had been defending Oscar, broke away and started running after Morgan!

She screamed and headed in the opposite direction. He continued after her, grinning, even though it was obvious that she wasn't enjoying this game of tag. Morgan cut this way and that, trying to avoid getting caught.

She screamed again. "Stop!" She had almost reached the far fence when I saw him tackle her. Morgan squirmed on the grass beneath him.

I sprinted toward them. "Get off her!"

Was he trying to kiss her? It was like I became the Incredible Hulk or something. I yanked him to his feet, then dropped him with a hammer-fist strike to the head.

Dwight David yelped.

An adult yelled out, "Stop! No fighting!"

Dwight David had fallen to his knees when I'd brought my fist down. Now he toppled, as if he were impersonating a dying cow. He rolled on the wet ground, moaning and groaning. *What a faker!*

The lady who had yelled, a seventh-grade teacher with a scary reputation, grabbed my arm and yanked me back. "I saw that. To the vice principal. *Now.*"

Vice Principal Bowman! I couldn't. Dad would kill me!

"But he jumped her!" I helped Morgan to her feet and pointed at Dwight David, who had stopped rolling and moaning while the teacher yelled at me, but now started up again.

"She tripped and I fell on her," Dwight David protested.

I looked to Morgan to confirm what he was saying, but she seemed too much in shock to answer.

"Ohhh . . . I think he broke my neck," Dwight David whined. He clutched his throat, and his face screwed up in what had to be mock pain. I hadn't clobbered him *that* hard. At least, I didn't think I had.

A bunch of kids crowded around, including Khal, Oscar, and Marcus. Even a few seventh graders.

"Isn't he the kid who broke your nose?" one of them asked Khal.

"Yeah! Jackie Chan!" another one said.

The teacher's eyes narrowed.

Weren't any of my friends going to stick up for me? I stared at Khal but he wouldn't look me in the eyes.

Morgan had her arms around her middle. Her freckles stood out even more than usual against her pale skin, which had gone ghostly.

"Back up, everyone. We'll let Mr. Bowman sort it out." The teacher put her hand on Morgan's shoulder and took me by the elbow. She looked at Khal and nodded toward Dwight David. "Help this boy to the office, will you? Everyone else, you've got three minutes left of free time. I recommend you get in out of the rain."

CHAPTER 25

I walked quickly alongside the teacher. There was no point in trying to make my case to her. She didn't want to hear it. I'd save my defense for Mr. Bowman, and boy, would I need a strong one. If he told Mom and Dad, I'd be grounded for the rest of my life.

I'd broken cardinal rule number one of Tae Kwon Do—the very first rule we learned as white belts and that we hear over and over again: Never use your abilities to attack or harm another. Truly strong Tae Kwon Do warriors promote nonviolence and do everything they can to avoid physical conflict. Dad had warned me that if I ever used Tae Kwon Do at school, the consequences would be severe.

I glanced over my shoulder. Dwight David hobbled along, leaning heavily on Khal. What an act. Was the kid trying to win an Academy Award?

I couldn't believe I was being sent to the vice principal. In elementary, the only times I'd been sent to the office were when the teacher asked me to pick up messages, and once to be congratulated for earning high marks in the fifth-grade science fair.

We took off our wet coats and waited in chairs along the wall while the teacher spoke with Mr. Bowman in his office. Morgan sat shivering next to me. Dwight David slouched a few seats away. Khal stood in the middle of the room, looking unsure of what to do. Finally, he sat on my other side.

"Why didn't you say anything out there?" I half-whispered.

"You kind of went ballistic, man," he whispered back.

"He attacked her!" I didn't bother trying to keep my voice down this time.

"You didn't have to go Tae Kwon Do on him."

Dwight David glared. "Yeah, you didn't have to go Tae Kwon Do on me!" His shoulders slumped even more. "Lola's gonna make me go to Mass every night for a week for getting sent to the vice principal again."

I glanced at Morgan, who looked about as comfortable as if she were sitting on a pincushion. She looked away. Was she mad at me, too?

"Anyway, I told you, she *tripped*," Dwight David said.

Morgan looked at him. "I wouldn't have, if you hadn't been *chasing* me."

"You actually tripped?" I said. Had I only seen what I wanted to?

The bell rang for fourth period. "Good luck," Khal said to me as he got up to go. "You're going to need it."

Suddenly, Vice Principal Bowman stood before us. The three of us sitting there sounded like a bullfrog choir. *Gulp. Gulp. Gulp.* The man was as tall as Dad, but wider, much wider, with a big, oval-shaped, shiny head— shiny as an eight ball, like he got up every morning and polished it along with his shiny black shoes. His eyes, cheeks, and lips sagged like a bulldog's. Hopefully that was the only reason kids called him Bowman the Bull-dog, and not because he tore into people and ripped them to shreds.

"Gentlemen," he said in a deep voice, "and young lady." He nodded toward Morgan, then gave me a look so piercing I thought I might turn to dust on the spot, as if his stare had special disintegration powers, like one of the X-Men or something. "Follow me, please."

I was so weak from fear, I wasn't sure my legs would hold me if I stood. *Baekjul boolgool.* Indomitable spirit. *Stay strong,* I told myself. Dwight David was the troublemaker. I'd just been defending an innocent person.

Your girlfriend, a voice in my head said.

Whoa, I said back, *no one said anything about her being my girlfriend.* So, I'd held her hand. Maybe I even liked her enough to ask her to be my girlfriend. But I'd defended her because it was the right thing to do.

Mr. Bowman pulled a chair into his office and set it next to the two already in front of his desk. "Have a seat, please." At least he was a polite X-Man bulldog. He skewered me with his stare again. "Mr. Buckley, is it?"

My heart palpitated. I was suddenly short of breath, but I found the strength to whisper, "Yes, sir."

"Can you please tell me what happened out there—"

"He hit me over the head!" Dwight David blurted out.

I glared at him across Morgan.

"Excuse me!" Mr. Bowman thundered. Dwight David shrank in his seat. "You will have your turn in due time, Mr. Del Santos." Mr. Bowman looked at me again. "Mr. Buckley?"

It felt as if we were sitting across from a judge, high on his judgment seat. Morgan stared straight ahead, looking as if she was trying not to cry. I swallowed again. "Dwight David was chasing Morgan. She kept telling him to stop. When he jumped on—"

"I *fell* on her."

"Jumped, fell, whatever—I ran over to . . ." I stopped. I didn't want it to sound like I was protecting my girlfriend.

But weren't you?

No!

"To *what*, Mr. Buckley?" Mr. Bowman clasped his hands on his desk.

"To . . . uh . . . to uphold justice!" I said triumphantly. Surely Mr. X-Man Vice Principal could appreciate that. I almost added that it was the Tae Kwon Do *way* to defend innocents, but decided it'd be better not to reveal I was a *you gup ja*, a black-belt-in-training.

Vice Principal Bowman's thick black eyebrows pulled together. "I see . . . And did you or did you not punch Mr. Del Santos in the head?"

"Well, not exactly. It's called a hammer-fist—"

Mr. Bowman cut me off with the death stare. He turned his attention to Dwight David. "What do you have to say for yourself, Mr. Del Santos? Was Miss"—he glanced at a paper on his desk—"Miss Belcher telling you to stop chasing her?"

Dwight David picked at his thumbnail. "I guess. . . ."

"And Miss Belcher, did Dwight David jump on you, or did you in fact trip, as he maintains?"

"I slipped on the grass. But still, he should have stopped when I told him to."

"You're absolutely correct. So, the first order of business is that you, Mr. Del Santos, need to offer this young lady an apology."

"I'm sorry," Dwight David mumbled.

Morgan turned and looked straight at Dwight David, even though he had his head down. "I accept."

Dwight David shifted uncomfortably. Was that it? He was off the hook, just like that?

Vice Principal Bowman put his pointer fingers together and touched them to his lips, as if he was thinking what to say next. His gaze landed on each of us, stopping with me. I quickly looked away—to a silver paddle hanging on the wall, engraved with two As and some symbol I didn't recognize. Vice principals weren't allowed to paddle kids anymore, were they?

"It's a little cold for the birds and the bees to be out, don't you think?"

The birds and the bees? What the heck was this guy talking about?

Hold on. I'd seen that phrase in the book Dad had handed me a few days before I boarded the *Olympus* with Morgan and her mom, about my body going through changes and starting to like girls.

"Let me give you a little advice, Mr. Del Santos, man to man, and as someone who was once eleven and full of pep and vinegar. Chasing a girl *will* get her attention. But showing courtesy and respect is going to get you a lot farther in the women department."

Morgan's cheeks turned as pink as Oscar's after he'd run the field.

Mr. Bowman was clearly implying that Dwight David chased Morgan down because he liked her. Dwight David was so kooky I could almost see it being true. And it *was* obvious that he liked her. He'd been acting like a lovestruck fool at the pizza party earlier. Then there'd been that behemoth bag of M&Ms a while ago, and of course, the dance.

"And, Brendan, although it was an honorable impulse on your part to defend Miss Belcher, you crossed the line when you acted aggressively toward your fellow classmate. You owe Mr. Del Santos an apology, as well."

Dwight David's lips turned up in a small smile.

It took all the *guk gi*—self-control—I could muster to say I was sorry. If only I'd shown a little more of it on the playing field. However, so far there'd been no talk of punishments. I wanted to get out of there before that changed. "Sorry, Dwight David."

"So, boys, what do you say you shake hands?"

Dwight David's head was still bowed. His hands stayed in his lap. I actually felt kind of sorry for him, if he didn't know how to get Morgan's attention any better than to hunt her down like a dog after a rabbit. I reached across Morgan.

Dwight David put his scrawny hand in mine. We shook.

"Let's keep it clean out there, what do you say?" We all nodded, even Morgan. "Report back here after school, Mr. Del Santos. You'll spend an hour in my office working on homework. I'll call your grandmother to let her know. Understood?"

Dwight David gasped. "What about him?" He pointed at me.

"*Understood?*"

"Yes, sir."

"You may leave."

Dwight David didn't waste any time. He was out the door in a flash. I stood to go.

"Not yet, Mr. Buckley."

My heart skipped a beat.

"I'd like to speak with you privately."

My armpits got hot.

Morgan hadn't moved.

"You may be excused, as well, Miss Belcher."

Morgan glanced at me, then at Mr. Bowman. She stood hesitantly. "Mr. Bowman, Brendan was just trying to defend—"

"Goodbye, Miss Belcher."

She closed her mouth. "See you later," she whispered. I nodded. She shut the door behind her.

Mr. Bowman's chair creaked as he leaned forward. His eyes penetrated my face. "I know your father."

My heart deflated like a punctured bike tire.

"We go way back. To our college days. We could have been great buddies, if he'd only pledged Alpha instead of Kappa." He glanced at the silver paddle. I knew that paddle had looked familiar! Dad had one like it, but wooden, and with different letters and symbols. A fraternity paddle.

The vice principal sat back, put his hands on his belly, and smiled wide. "So, how is old Sam?"

Was that it—the reason he wanted to speak with me in private? The sweat under my arms started to cool. "He's good." I allowed myself to smile, too. "He's a detective in the Tacoma Police Department."

"It's detective now, eh? I saw his name in an article last year. A big drug bust, wasn't it?"

"Yes, sir." Dad's role in the bust had been the reason he got promoted.

"I'm sorry he and I will be getting back in touch under such unfortunate circumstances."

I stared at him. "What do you mean?" I asked, even though it was pretty clear what he meant.

"I mean, if your dad is as serious about his standards for his son as he was for himself when I knew him, I don't think he's going to be too happy to get my call."

"Do you have to call him?" My voice came out as a squeak.

"I'm sorry to say I do." Mr. Bowman put his elbows on his desk. "Brendan, look. You're obviously a very bright kid. You were just named a finalist in a national science competition. Congratulations for that, by the way."

"Thanks." I looked down.

"So, how about the next time you want to defend a girl, you use your brain and your words instead of your fists?"

"Okay." I looked up and added quickly, "Sir."

"Good. But I still have to call your parents. It's district policy. Along with a minimum one-day suspension for physical violence."

My heart dropped into my shoes. *Suspension!*

"I'll speak with your parents to determine the best day for you to stay home. You'll be allowed to request assignments from teachers in advance so your absence won't impede your academic progress."

Suspension.

The word felt like cement blocks on my feet. Mom would at least give me a chance to explain, but Dad was going to kill me.

CHAPTER 26

For the next three periods, I kept to myself. I put off Morgan's and Khal's questions about what had happened in Bowman's office with promises to tell them later. At the sound of the final bell, I made a beeline for my locker, hoping to get out of there before I saw anyone.

"Brendan, what *happened?*" Morgan stood too close. "Are you in trouble?" I bent down and dug around for my gym shorts. "What did he *say?*"

I stuffed the shorts into my duffel bag. *Might as well tell her—she's going to find out eventually.* "I've been suspended."

"Suspended!" Her eyes opened wide. Her face looked pale again. "But Dwight David started the whole thing. That's not fair!"

The hallway was crowded with kids jostling and shouting on their way to the exits, like blood cells in an artery. I stepped back to shut my locker. Morgan grabbed my hand. "Oh, Brendan. I'm so sorry. Can your parents contest it?"

I felt like a lobster that had just been dunked in boiling water. I glanced around. Luckily, no one seemed to be noticing me standing there with a girl holding my hand.

*Un*luckily, Khalfani appeared, clutching his football. "What are you doing, man? We're waiting for you." He spied our hands and made a face. I broke free.

"I have to go." I lowered my voice. "I've been suspended."

"*What?* No way!" Khal said.

Morgan reached out for my arm. "Maybe if I talk to Mr. Bowman again . . ."

"*No.*" I pulled away but tried to make it seem as if I were just throwing my duffel bag over my shoulder, not avoiding her. I kept my eyes on my bag. My ears were still warm from being caught with my hand in hers. "It was my fault. I didn't have to clobber him."

Morgan's eyes got big and dreamy, like a puppy's. "Maybe so. But still, it *was* really great of you to stand up for me like that." Her lips pushed out a little.

She wasn't about to try to kiss me again, was she? I stepped back to prevent any lip action, in case that was what she had in mind.

"So, like, do you have to get off school property immediately?" Khal asked. "Because we need five players, and I already convinced Dwight David to play on the same team as you."

"I don't know. I just know I have to get to my parents before Vice Principal Bowman does. Ask Cordé. He's better than me, anyway."

"He hogs the ball."

"You only think that because *you* hog the ball." I felt jumpy and irritated, like a bull with too many flies buzzing around his face. If I stood there one second longer, I might start bucking. I started walking instead.

"Can I call you later?" Morgan asked.

"Are you going to Tae Kwon Do tonight?" Khalfani called.

"I don't know," I shouted over my shoulder. And I really didn't. I didn't know anything except that I was about to get it. *Big*-time.

———————

When I got home, there was a note on the fridge from Mom. She'd gone out Christmas shopping. "P.S. Bringing home teriyaki for dinner ☺!" she'd written.

I crumpled the note and threw it in the trash. I'd been hoping she'd be there so I could explain things to her first. Then she could act as a neutralizer when Dad had the big reaction over my being suspended.

I stayed in my room all afternoon, observing Einstein and trying not to think about what would happen when Dad got home. I was concerned about my lizard.

For the last week or so, he'd been sluggish. He didn't pounce on the crickets as soon as they landed; he'd just watch as they hopped away. His eyes were sunken in and half-closed most of the time.

I opened the lid and pushed back the plant leaves. Einstein lay on the jungle vine. He didn't even seem to notice my hand as I gently lifted him from the tank.

He felt limp. His skin looked dull. I examined him more closely. Some strange spots had appeared. I stroked his back a few times. "What's wrong, little buddy? Are you sick?" I set him gently back on his rock, checked the tank temps, and squirted the leaves a couple of times.

As soon as the lid was back on, I went to my desk and got online. I needed to find out what was wrong with Einstein. An hour later, I had a sinking feeling it might be parasites. Parasites, according to the forum posts I read, were best treated by a reptile vet. And even then, a parasite-ridden anole had a very slim chance of making it.

There was no way Dad would agree to take Einstein back to the vet. Not after the bill we'd gotten for his first checkup. And especially not after he found out I was suspended. I wasn't going to be getting any special favors for a very long time.

I went back to Einstein's tank. Why had I fed him those spiders? That was the most likely cause of the problem, since they hadn't been bred in some store. *Stupid.*

A car door slammed outside. The front door opened and shut. "Brendan!" Something told me Dad had heard from Mr. Bowman already.

I came out from my room, even though I wanted to be like Einstein and find a good place to hide.

Dad paced in the living room. "Sit," he said as soon as he saw me.

I perched on the love seat.

"I got a call from your vice principal."

Now probably wasn't the best time to inquire about their college days.

"You going to tell me what happened?"

I cleared my throat. "Um . . . well, see . . . this kid was harassing Morgan." Dad had once used the same word to describe how a female detective was getting treated at work. He'd been really ticked about it.

"And hitting him was the answer?"

"He was *attacking* her."

"Huh." Dad crossed his arms. "That's a pretty different account from what I heard. Sounded to me like the kid made a fumble and you sacked him after the whistle had blown."

"Morgan's not a football!"

Dad looked at me intently, his jaw clenched tight. He sat in the armchair. "Look, Brendan, I'm sure you meant well. But you overreacted. You hammer-fisted a kid for chasing a girl. And you used your Tae Kwon Do at school. Something we agreed you'd never do."

I had no defense against those charges.

"Is this boy as big as you, at least?"

I shook my head. "He's kind of small, actually." A wave of shame washed over me. I'd really messed up.

"What's gotten into you?" Dad sounded exasperated. "First, excessive force with Khalfani, and now this?"

I shrugged. Did Dad want me to be tough or didn't he? I guessed hitting a kid who was smaller than me didn't fit into Dad's definition of toughness. If I was honest, it didn't fit into mine, either. But what *did* it mean to be tough? And did I or did I not need to be it?

"Well, you'll have plenty of time to think about it on Thursday." Dad exhaled. "Go to your room. We'll talk more about this later."

"Yes, sir."

I went and sat at my desk. I stared at my open math book, but all I could think about was my dad. I'd let him down. Not just by hitting Dwight David over the head. It was more than that. Something about myself. Who I was. Or wasn't.

I would never be the superjock baseball or football player. I didn't want to raid drug houses or put people in jail, even people who deserved it.

I liked *thinking* about stuff, and learning about things, like supernovas, and phytoplankton, and subterranean microbes that ate rocks far below the Earth's crust and kept the cycle of life going. I liked doing experiments with cow manure.

I was all right with that. I knew Mom was, too. But was Dad? Would he ever be?

I got busy working on my math assignment. Compared to my dad and me, these problems would be a breeze.

CHAPTER 27

Mom, Dad, and I had our "big conversation" over teriyaki that night. Not wanting to get into everything again, I told them right away that I knew I was in the wrong and they didn't need to worry about me doing anything like that ever again.

Dad said, "Good," thumped me on the back a couple of times, then shoveled down his food and rushed out the door for class. I got out of Tae Kwon Do by saying I felt sick, which I did. Sick to my stomach.

The morning of my suspension, first Morgan called, and then Khal. It was nice to know I had friends.

I hung up the phone after telling Khal I'd see him Friday. "Hey, Boo," Mom said, coming into the kitchen. "Ready for breakfast?" Mom didn't work on

Thursdays. She'd already told me she planned to be home with me all day. I glanced at the clock: 8:20. I'd been so busy talking to my friends, I hadn't given Einstein his crickets.

"After I feed Einstein," I said, heading for my room.

"How about eggs and bacon?" Mom called.

"Sure!" I hollered. I turned on my bedroom light. "Guess what, Einstein? I get to stay home with you today." Einstein lay in a corner with his back against the glass. I'd never seen him lie in that spot before. "Einstein?" He was too still. "Einstein!" I snatched off the lid and peered over the edge. His eyes were closed. He didn't move.

I reached in and touched him with the end of my pointer finger. He still didn't move. His long tail drooped as I lifted his lifeless body from the tank.

I dropped to the floor, cradling my anole in my palms. Crickets hopped around inside the cricket carrier under the card table. They would live to see another day, but not my lizard. Einstein was gone.

———

Mom and I stood outside in our backyard, white puffs appearing in front of our faces whenever we exhaled. It started to drizzle. I clutched the shoe box that held Einstein, along with some orchid bark, a couple of crickets (they'd feed off his body before dying themselves, helping him to decompose more quickly), and one of the quartz crystals I'd found on the dig back in August.

Mom held out the shovel. "You want to do the honors?"

I gave her the box and took the shovel. I stabbed the hard ground, then pushed on the edge of the spade with my foot. This was going to take a while.

As the hole got bigger, I started to think about last spring. Being at the cemetery. Sitting on a hard folding chair at the side of that huge dug-out rectangle. Listening to the sound of some lady singing: *God has smiled on me. He has set me free.* . . . Feeling Mom tremble next to me. Hearing Gladys's choked cries as she muttered, *My Clem.* . . . Watching a single tear trickle down Dad's wooden cheek on its way to his clenched jaw.

Why did everything die? I knew there was a scientific explanation, but I didn't care. It wasn't right. It shouldn't be this way.

I dropped the shovel and looked at Mom. Her eyes squinted and her lips turned down. "Sorry, Boo," she said, handing me the box.

My fingers were stiff and achy, but I grasped the box tightly. I faced the hole. "You were a great pet and a good friend. I'm sorry we didn't get to know each other for longer." I crouched and set the box in the hole, remembering how those strangers had lowered Grampa Clem's coffin into the dug-out rectangle. We passed by, one by one, tossing in flowers that had been handed to us.

I looked around Mom's flower beds but there were no flowers in December. I pulled up a handful of wet grass, sprinkled it on top of the box, and then shoveled the dirt back into the hole.

When it was done, we went inside. Dad would probably be annoyed that Einstein was dead after just four months, but I didn't care. He could be annoyed all he wanted. I was still going to miss my lizard.

Log Entry—Friday, December 7

Home from school. It wasn't as bad as I thought it would be—going back. Lauren Dweck asked me if I was feeling better. That's when I discovered that Khal told everyone I was sick.

Of course, Gladys and Grandpa Ed knew the truth. I told them, since I figured they'd find out anyway. Gladys tried to convince Dad that she needed me to go with her to the podiatrist on the day of my suspension, but she didn't really. She was just trying to get me out of the house. Spending an afternoon looking at Gladys's feet is really the last thing I'd ever want to do, but in the end, it would have been better than sitting in my room all day without Einstein. My room's just not the same without him.

Khal, Morgan, and Gladys have all told me I can get another anole, and Grandpa Ed has already

offered to buy me one, but I can't just replace
Einstein like that. Then again, Grandpa Ed got a new
dog after the original Patches died from a raccoon
attack, and that's why he has P.J.—Patches Junior.

Hmm... Einstein Junior. I kind of like the sound
of that!

CHAPTER 28

The following week, Mr. Hammond asked Morgan and me to stay after class. "Do you think he's got news about the contest?" Morgan whispered excitedly from her seat behind me. Khal and I still sat at the same table, but right then he was leaning over to Cordé talking about something.

"That's got to be it!" I said, starting to get the Jitters.

Shyla-Ann giggled a few seats away. Dwight David, who'd been hanging around her more and more the last few days, had apparently done something funny.

The bell rang and Mr. H handed out our final exam for the quarter. Winter break started this weekend. I was so ready—for the break and for our science test. I breezed through the questions, turned in my test, and had fifteen minutes left to read *Percy Jackson*.

When time was up, Mr. Hammond asked those still

working to hand in their papers. "How'd you do?" I asked Khal as he got up to go to the front.

"I may not be a scientific genius like you or Morgan." His eyes slid over to where Morgan sat. "But I did all right, I think."

"Hey, I have an idea!" Morgan said. "We could form a team of three for next year's contest. What do you think, Khalfani?" She always used his full name. "Brendan and I have already begun thinking about what we're going to do. Probably something related to deep-sea exploration."

Khal looked doubtful. He still wasn't sure whether Morgan was someone he could be friends with. "I don't know. Maybe . . . it *sounds* cool."

"Tests in, please," Mr. H called again. Kids filed out the door. We said goodbye to Khal and went to the front of the room to wait for whatever Mr. Hammond had to tell us.

When everyone was gone, Mr. H turned to us. "So."

I could see it on his face. "We didn't win, did we?" I said.

"You didn't win first place."

My shoulders dropped.

Mr. H looked us in the eyes. "But you still won."

Morgan nodded. "That's true. It's a really big deal that we were regional finalists."

"Absolutely," Mr. Hammond agreed. "Not to mention you've both earned a science kit of your choice and three hundred dollars to spend on our classroom. I'm grateful for that!"

I knew they were right, but I was disappointed anyway. I'd been hoping to win a trip to MIT. "Who got the top prize?" I asked.

"A team from Louisiana. For a project on algae blooms in the Gulf of Mexico."

"Algae," I said, looking at Morgan. "That's what you proposed."

"It doesn't matter, Brendan. What we did was great—and important. And we had a lot of fun together." She looked at me out of the corner of her eye and smiled. "Didn't we?"

I was starting to get a little hot under my sweater. "Yeah, I guess."

Mr. H put his hand on my shoulder. "There's always next year, bud."

At home, I lay on my bed watching my solar-system mobile spin slowly from the air blowing through the vent. I glanced at Einstein's empty tank. I had told Grandpa Ed I wanted another anole after all—once I got over Einstein, of course.

My mind returned to the contest. I'd really hoped we'd win the whole thing, mainly because it would be awesome, but also so that Dad would see that this science "stuff" *was* worth my time. Would I tell him about it when he got home? Would he even care?

A weight settled on me. Not *on* me, exactly, as if an elephant were sitting on my chest. More like *in* me. My legs, torso, and arms felt as if they'd been injected with lead. I had *become* heaviness. *Maybe this is what it feels like to be a hundred feet under the ocean*, I thought. The opposite of being in outer space. *Sub*gravity. Being pulled toward the Earth's core so forcefully that you can't lift your body if you try. Morgan had told me she wanted to be a geobiologist, a scientist who studies the connection between rocks and life, exploring the rocks below the deep sea floor. She was brave. I didn't think I could handle being that far under water.

I thought of Grandpa Ed again. He knew how important this contest had been to me. He would understand.

Six months ago, I hadn't known my grandpa's phone number or where he lived. Or even if he was alive. I had never spoken to him. Not once. Things sure had changed.

I got the phone and came back to my room. I speed-dialed his number.

"Yell-o."

"It's me."

"Well, hello, me. Good to hear from you. To what do I owe the pleasure?"

"Nothing, really. I just wanted to say hi."

"That's good enough reason in my book. So, what have you been up to?"

"Not much. Studying. Homework." I paused. "We didn't win the national prize."

Grandpa Ed was silent for a moment. "I thought your voice was lacking its usual luster. Pretty disappointed, huh?"

I sighed and bent my knees. "Yeah, I am." I put my free hand behind my head. I suddenly didn't feel so heavy. As if having someone acknowledge that the science contest was important enough to be disappointed about had helped me not be so disappointed. And really, it *was* a huge honor even to get to the regional level.

"What'd your parents say?"

"I haven't seen them yet. Dad probably won't say anything."

"What makes you think that?"

"I don't know . . . he just doesn't seem to care about what I care about."

"Hmm . . . have you told him that?"

I thought for a moment. "I guess not."

"Well, maybe you should. Give him a chance. You did that for me, and look how well that turned out."

I supposed he had a point.

"Listen, son. You did a great job on your project. No one else in your school got chosen as a regional finalist."

"No other sixth graders in the whole state of Washington," I reminded him.

"Exactly! Plus, you learned how to make something useful out of waste. And, if I remember correctly, you had more questions when you finished than when you started, isn't that right?"

"Right."

"Well then, as your fellow scientist, I declare your venture into the world of biofuels a verifiable success!"

Talking to Grandpa Ed had helped me feel better about things, but I still had a hard time imagining that Dad would ever see it the way my grandpa did, no matter how much I wanted him to.

CHAPTER 29

A few days before Christmas, Mom and Dad held a party at our house. Khalfani's family had been on the invite list from the beginning. When Mom suggested adding Morgan and her parents, I didn't try to change her mind.

I had told my parents about not winning the national prize, of course. Mom had made a big deal about how winning wasn't the most important thing—it was the experience, what I'd learned, and all that. She was still very proud of me, she said. Dad had pointed out that only one team could win top prize and the odds of that happening for anyone were very slim. I hadn't tried to talk to him any more about it.

"The grandparents here yet?" Dad asked, coming into the dining area, where Mom had arranged a bunch of food on the table. She started to light the candles.

"Can I do it?" I loved using the lighter.

Mom handed it to me. "Dad said they'd be here by four."

Grandpa Ed was bringing Gladys. They'd been doing more together lately, ever since a recent Sunday dinner when he'd invited her to a movie. "No need for us both to be sitting home alone," he'd said.

"Speak for yourself. I like being alone." Gladys had sat up tall and thrust out her chin. "But I'll go. Maybe that pest Bernard will finally leave me alone if he sees you hanging around."

"I doubt it." Grandpa Ed had chuckled. "You're a hot item, Gladys. You know that."

"And you're full of it, Rock Hudson."

I lit the final candle as Grandpa Ed's truck pulled up outside. I would've recognized that sputtering sound anywhere. I ran to the window. "They're here!" I called.

My jaw dropped. Gladys was getting out on the driver's side! Gladys didn't drive. She was always bragging about being "all bus, all the time."

"Mom! Dad! Gladys drove Grandpa Ed's truck!"

Dad came up behind me. "God help us all."

Gladys and Grandpa Ed were laughing and carrying on as if they were best friends.

Mom opened the door. "I see you've decided to take up driving again."

"I sure have!" Gladys said. She practically hopped up the stairs. "Thanks to Ed here." She turned and smiled down at him. Then she waved her hands in the air and did a little dance around the living room. "Get ready, everybody, 'cause here I come!"

"Watch out, everybody, is more like it." Dad shook his head. "Ed, I thought you were more sensible than that. Don't you know a car can be considered a lethal weapon in a court of law?"

Gladys scowled.

Grandpa Ed appeared at the top of the stairs. "Your mom did just fine. Handled my old truck the way she handles everything—she let it know who was boss right from the start."

Gladys smiled again. "Thank you, Edwin."

"Just remember, I warned you," Dad said.

"Grandpa Ed's a good teacher," I said, thinking of the time he'd let me drive his truck on a deserted back road this past summer. Mom looked at me funny. "At least when it comes to things like geology and chess," I added quickly. I'd never told my parents about Grandpa Ed putting me behind the wheel. "So he's probably good at teaching driving, too."

"You pick out your science kit for winning that contest yet?" Grandpa Ed handed Mom his coat. I had been given a choice of over twenty kits from an online company.

"There's one on genetics and DNA that looks cool. I think I might get that one."

"We don't need to do any DNA tests to know where

you got your science smarts," Gladys said, putting her arm around me.

"That's right!" Grandpa Ed said. "Like I've said before, Brendan's a chip off this old rock." He knocked my shoulder with his fist.

Gladys scoffed. "That may be so, Rock, but it wasn't you I was referring to. My Clem had dreams of being a surgeon one day."

"He did?" I said, astonished. "Grampa Clem never told me that."

Dad's forehead creased. "I never heard that, either."

"You didn't know *everything* about the man." Gladys looked at Dad over the rims of her pointy glasses; then she turned back to me. "Circumstances beyond his control landed him in X-rays. But your grandpa had a keen scientific mind. So you got it from both sides, Mr. Science Genius!"

The doorbell rang. I went to answer it, still pondering this new information I'd been given about my family tree. Khal and his stepmom were at the door. Khal's dad was helping Dori out of the car.

"Hey, Brendan." Khal came inside and took off his shoes.

Khal's stepmom held a casserole dish covered in foil. "Hello, Brendan."

"Peach cobbler?" I asked, taking the warm bowl in my hands and inhaling the delicious, sweet smell.

"Don't you know it," she said.

I licked my lips. Mrs. Jones's peach cobbler was *incredible*.

Dori pushed her way inside. "Look at what I got, Brendan!" She held up a brown-skinned doll with three thick braids exactly like hers. The doll wore a red and black dress with white tights and black shoes just like Dori, too. "A My Twinn doll!" She ran up the stairs and started telling Mom about the doll.

Khal rolled his eyes. "She's been wearing that same outfit since her birthday *eight days* ago. I think she's going for a world record."

"Khalfani Omar," Mrs. Jones said with a warning tone in her voice. Mr. Jones came in carrying a bag of wrapped gifts. He and Mrs. Jones headed upstairs. Khal and I went down to the rec room to play Nintendo baseball.

A little while later, the doorbell rang again. I heard Mom open the door and greet Morgan and her parents.

Khal made a face. "Of course you'd invite your girl-friend."

I ran my player around the bases. "My mom invited them." Khal didn't need to know I'd been glad about it. "You could give her a chance, you know." Saying that made me think of Grandpa Ed's words to me about Dad. I pushed the thought away.

"Me being friends with the Belcher is about as likely as my sister never bugging me again."

I glanced up just as Morgan appeared in the doorway.

"Hi, Brendan. Hi, Khalfani." She came and stood nearby.

I said hi, but I kept my eyes on the TV. What was Morgan to me, anyway? *Was* she my girlfriend? We'd never said anything about being boyfriend and girlfriend. We'd just spent a whole lot of time together, maybe even more than Khal and I had so far this year. Did that make us an official couple?

What about the fact that I looked forward to seeing her at our lockers first thing in the morning, or that I hoped when the phone rang after school that it was her, or that I had started to worry that we wouldn't see each other as much now that the contest was over?

What about the flutters I had in my stomach right then as I looked up and saw her big brown eyes and the cute freckles on her nose and the dimple in her cheek? What about *that*?

I quickly put my eyes back on the game. "Ohh!" I shouted as Khal tagged my runner out at home plate.

"I guess I'll see you upstairs," Morgan said, turning toward the door.

I glanced up. "Okay," I said, even though I'd been hoping she would stay to watch me play.

A while later, Dad came in. He started shoveling through boxes in the corner of the room. "Khal, would you believe your dad's not buying that I have a baseball signed by all the Griffeys—Ken Senior, Ken Junior, and the younger one, Craig, the one who played for the Rainiers?"

Khal jumped up and ran to the corner. "You do?"

"I'm going to get something to eat," I said, even though Khal wasn't listening and I wasn't actually hungry.

Upstairs, Christmas music played on the stereo. The living room had gotten crowded with all the guests, people I recognized but didn't really know from both Mom's and Dad's workplaces, and some of their friends from the neighborhood. I wound around the small groups of people standing and eating off small paper plates. No Morgan. She wasn't in the dining area or the kitchen, either.

I started down the hall. My bedroom door, which I remembered having closed on purpose, was cracked. Was Morgan in my room? A bunch of thoughts flooded my mind at once: *She can't just go into my room without me! Did I pick up my dirty underwear? But if she feels comfortable enough to go into my room, then we must be pretty good friends. Maybe even best friends. You can't be best friends with a girl!* My thoughts made me feel all jumbled up inside, like a scrambled radio signal.

I peered through the opened door. Morgan stood looking down at my desk, on top of which sat my logbook!

I burst into the room. "That's private!" I cried.

She spun around, eyes wide. Her face turned pinker

by the second. "I—I didn't look. I would never look." She started to rush past me out the door.

"Wait." I pulled her back inside and shut the door. When I turned around, we were about a centimeter from each other's faces. I cleared my throat and stepped back.

She looked down. "I'm sorry. I shouldn't have come into your room without asking. I just wanted to see Einstein's tank . . . one last time." She looked at me earnestly. "I swear I would never look at your journal."

"It's a logbook," I said.

"Right. Your logbook."

This is it, I thought. *My chance.* I would make it official. Right then. I would ask Morgan if she wanted to be my girlfriend. It didn't matter what Khal thought.

"Mor—"

"I've been—"

"Would you—"

"Maybe we—"

If we had been at a dance we would've been stepping all over each other's feet.

"You can go first," I said, trying to be gentlemanly, like Gladys had told me to be after sitting next to Morgan at the tournament. "Here." I gestured toward my outer space bedspread.

Morgan pulled in her bottom lip. She went and sat on Jupiter. "I'm really glad we got partnered together for the science contest," she said.

"Yeah," I said, sitting on the sun. I held on to the

bedpost as if I were afraid a black hole might open between us and suck us in. I kept hearing the sentence Mr. H had taught us to help us memorize the order of the planets: *Mary's violet eyes make John stay up nights permanently.* (Pluto is no longer considered the ninth planet, of course, but he still wanted us to learn it as a dwarf planet.)

Instead of hearing *Mary's*, though, I heard *Morgan's*, and I wasn't just *thinking* about her eyes, like that John guy. I was staring into them.

Morgan's velvet eyes make Jupiter silly. . . .

I shook my head, which had clouded over like a Puget Sound fog. What was wrong with me? *Pull yourself together, man!*

"I've been wondering," Morgan continued. "I mean . . . we've been spending a lot of time together."

"Yeah, I know." Maybe this wouldn't be so hard after all. It sounded as if she was headed in the same direction I'd been planning to go.

"I was thinking . . ."

"Me too!" I said.

She blinked a few times. "Really? You were wondering if we should spend less time together so we don't end up not having any other friends?"

"Oh." The disappointed sound came out before I could stop it. It felt as if someone had hammer-fisted *me* on the head this time.

Morgan's eyes got even rounder than usual. "That's not what you were thinking, was it?"

I nodded quickly. "No—I mean, yes! You're exactly right." I rubbed my sweaty palms on my pants, trying to think of what to say. "I've been thinking I need to start hanging more with my friends. You know, Khal and Oscar and Marcus. They're my crew, after all." I looked at her out of the corner of my eye, then back at my hands.

"Right. Your crew." She traced Saturn's rings with her finger. "Do you consider me a friend, too?"

"Um . . ." I had a sick feeling in my stomach. This was not going well at all.

"That's okay. I understand. You were just being nice because I was new and all that. You probably only spent time with me because you wanted to win the competition. And on the boat"—it was the first time either of us had mentioned that day since it'd happened—"we were just caught up in the excitement of learning we'd been chosen as finalists, right?" She stood as if she was planning to leave.

I grabbed her wrist. "Wait! That's not it at all."

She pulled her hand away and crossed her arms over her stomach.

"I mean, maybe at first I was just being nice. And of course I wanted to win. But I *do* like you. You're smart and funny . . . and, and . . ."

I heard Khal's voice in my head. *Where's your* baekjul boolgool, *man?*

"And I liked holding your hand." I said it quickly, then looked over at Einstein's tank. It was so quiet I thought I could hear the beads of sweat popping from my forehead.

Morgan sat again—on Venus this time. "I liked holding your hand, too."

"Do you want to hold hands now?" I asked.

"Sure."

We reached across Mercury. Our fingers had just touched when someone knocked on the door. We jerked our hands back into our laps, as if we'd been burned by the planet's hot gases.

"Brendan, you in there?" Dad called.

"Yes," I said, trying to sound as casual as possible, even though every molecule in my body was ricocheting around from the heat of the last few moments.

"It's time to play the game," Dad said. "You and your friends going to join us?"

"Sure. Be there in a minute."

I looked at Morgan, then took her hand again, hoping mine didn't feel too sweaty. "I have something for you," I said. Grandpa Ed and I had spent some extra time in the lapidary shop over the past few weeks. He'd shown me how to cut and polish a cabochon—or cab, as they were called in the rock club world. I hadn't been exactly sure who I was making it for, but right then, I knew.

"Ooh, a surprise. I love surprises."

"Me too," I said, thinking about how surprising it was to be sitting on my bed holding a girl's hand.

"Soooo?" she said, glancing around.

"Oh, right." I jumped up and went to my desk. I pulled out the middle drawer and found the rose quartz cab—flat on the bottom, concave across the top, and shaped like a heart.

When I turned she was standing in the middle of the room.

"Here," I said, thrusting it at her before I lost my nerve. "This is for you."

Her eyes opened wide. She beamed and grasped the pink stone to her chest. Then she pecked me on the cheek. "It's *beautiful*! I love it. Thank you." She gazed at the heart again, smiling.

I had a feeling there would be more hand-holding in Morgan's and my future, and that made me smile, too.

CHAPTER 30

Christmas morning, I woke up with a strange feeling in my stomach. It wasn't hunger, even though Mom's sticky buns already filled the air with a fantastic cinnamony smell. And it wasn't eagerness to get to the presents.

It was sadness.

December 25 was Grampa Clem's birthday. He'd always taken pride in being born on the same day as Jesus.

I'd known it was coming, of course. Dad had been talking to Gladys for a while about visiting the cemetery on Christmas Day. I didn't know if they were going or not, but if they did, I wasn't going with them. That filled-in hole just held some old skin and bones—not my Grampa Clem.

There was a knock on my door. I pushed myself up in bed and rubbed my eyes. "Come in," I said.

Dad poked his head in. "You up?" he asked. A few

years back, I would have been up at the crack of dawn, bouncing on my parents' bed, begging to open presents. But not anymore.

"Yeah," I said. "Just thinking."

"Oh yeah? 'Bout what?" Dad stepped into the room and flipped on the light. He held something long and skinny wrapped in garbage bags.

"Grampa Clem."

"Mmm." He glanced at the shelf over Einstein's tank. "That's quite a collection you've got going."

"Twenty-two specimens," I said. "Nothing close to Grandpa Ed's, though."

Dad picked up a quartz crystal from the dig back in August. "Is this one of the rocks I found in the garbage?"

I felt my face scrunch. "*You* put those back on my desk?"

"Who'd you think did?"

I shrugged. "Mom."

Dad nodded. "I can see why you might think that." He looked at the crystal more closely. "I found them when I was emptying your trash can. Didn't think they belonged there." He put the quartz back on the shelf. "So, you ready to open your first present?" He held out the long, skinny whatever-it-was.

As soon as I grasped it in my hand, I knew. A fishing pole.

I pulled off the top bag and shook the rod free. "Grampa Clem's pole," I said, my heart starting to thump. "I wondered what Gladys had done with it . . . I didn't want to ask."

"It's yours now," Dad said. He put his hands on my shoulders. They didn't feel like weights this time. More like Khal's football pads. "My dad might not have been a very large man, but he sure left a large hole."

My heart squeezed. "Yeah," I said.

Dad pulled me into his chest. My eyes started to sting, but I swallowed it all back down.

He made space between us again. "Every day I find myself thinking about what he'd say about this or that, wishing he could see me finishing my degree. . . ."

I'd heard Dad say that all sons wanted their dads' approval, but I'd never thought about that including him.

I looked for the scratch on the soft handle from when Grampa Clem almost lost his pole off the pier. The big fish that had nearly pulled the pole—and Grampa Clem—over the railing had gotten away, of course.

"How'd you like to go fishing this morning, before we open the rest of the presents?"

I smiled. "Really? That would be great."

"All right. Get yourself ready and we'll get out of here." He slapped me on the back and started to leave the room.

"Dad—" I swallowed. I was a scientist unsure about what to do or the outcome of my next step.

Dad stood in the doorway.

"Do you think I'm weird . . . ?"

Dad's eyebrows pulled together.

"I mean, for liking science and . . . and school?"

He drew his chin into his chest. "Why would you think that?" He stepped back into the room and pushed the door almost closed.

"I heard you talking to Mom." I bit on the inside of my lip. "You called me an egghead."

Dad's jaw went slack. "Oh." He looked at the floor, then peered at me through squinty eyes. He studied me as if I were a page in one of his books and he was having a hard time with the subject. "Look, Bren, I didn't mean . . . I mean, there's nothing wrong with being good at school."

"But you think I should be tougher."

Dad pointed to the bed and we sat, side by side.

"Your grampa was a strong, proud, tough man. *Too* tough on me and my brother, at times. Seemed like all he cared about was me getting better grades than I ever could, ever did. I worked so hard to make him proud . . . in baseball, at the academy. But it never seemed to be good enough." Dad looked down at his hands—open, empty.

"Your grampa was not a perfect man, Bren. And I'm not, either. I've been too hard on you at points, just like my dad was too hard on me." Dad put his hand on my shoulder and gazed at my face. "The last thing I want is for you to feel like I did—like you're always coming up short. . . . I couldn't ask for a better son." His eyes started to water and he looked away. The words that came next came out as a whisper, but I heard them loud and clear: "I love you, you know."

I put my arm around his back and held on. "I love you, too, Dad. And I'm really proud of you for going back to school."

Later, as we left the house, I pictured myself sitting on Dad's lap behind the wheel of his parked patrol car. It was something we'd done a lot when I was little, but I hadn't thought about it in a long time. Dad would turn on the siren and we'd pretend we were chasing bad guys. I was going to be a police officer, just like him.

"Dad?"

"Yes."

"Remember how I used to pretend to drive your patrol car?"

"Sure do."

"That was fun."

"Yep. It was." Dad loaded the poles and Grampa Clem's tackle box in the back of his Chevy Blazer and we got in. He sat with his hands on the wheel, but he didn't turn the key. "I don't expect you to be a police officer, Brendan. I expect you to be whatever it is you're good at."

I swallowed. "Okay." And it was okay, because I knew he really meant it.

Dad started the motor. "Oh, and by the way, being tough means you're not going to let anyone stop you from doing what you need to do, or being who you need to be—not even your old man." As he looked over his shoulder to back out of the driveway, he smiled.

I smiled back.

CHAPTER 31

We were the only ones out on the frosty pier. As we listened to water lap the pylons and waited for something to bite, Dad told me something else I'd never known about Grampa Clem. He'd never taken my dad fishing. "Too busy working, trying to save up for his sons' college education."

Hearing that made me grateful for the times Dad, Mom, and I had gone camping or to California to visit my cousins. Dad worked a lot, but at least until he'd started school this fall, he'd still had time to do fun things together. And his classes wouldn't last forever. Apparently, Grampa Clem hadn't had the same opportunity until later in his life—after I'd come along.

Dad also told me stories about when he had graduated from elementary to middle school. "I remember it felt like going from Little League to the majors," he said.

"I was afraid I'd get stuffed in a locker, or depantsed in the middle of a crowded hallway, or older boys would gang up on me and force me to take drugs."

Being forced to use drugs? I'd never even thought to be afraid of that, although I knew some kids did experiment with that stuff. Talk about a dumb experiment.

"I got picked on a lot in sixth grade because I wore glasses. I was an easy target, being so scrawny and all."

My eyes opened wide. "You? Scrawny?"

"I didn't get tall until high school. That's also when I started building up my biceps . . . mostly for baseball, but I didn't mind the attention from the girls, either." We grinned at each other.

I told him about sitting in Bulldog Bowman's office feeling sure I'd be pulverized into dust by his X-Man stare, and about Morgan and me. "I really like her, Dad," I admitted.

"She seems like quite the catch." He looked at me out of the corner of his eye and smiled.

We were quiet for a while. Just like Grampa Clem and I used to be. Then he told me about a time earlier that month when he'd come down to the pier, trying to feel closer to his dad. "I found a man passed out, drunk. I thought, *This guy must have lost something or someone he really loved*." Dad had driven him to a shelter and left some money in his coat pocket for when he woke up.

I hadn't known my dad would do something like that.

Back in the car, Dad asked, "So, when do you think houses in Washington will start getting heated with this biogas stuff?"

I told him everything I knew, everything I'd learned from doing our experiment. He listened and asked lots of great questions—all the way home.

―――――

We returned cold and without any fish, but it had been a good time. Dad said we could even make it an annual Christmas tradition if I wanted, in honor of Grampa Clem.

Inside, the house smelled like bacon and pine branches and hot apple cider. Mom came to the top of the stairs wearing her apron. "Breakfast is ready whenever you are," she said. "Did you have any luck out there?"

I shook my head as I went up the stairs. "Nope. But it was a lot of fun."

Gladys and Grandpa Ed sat at the table playing chess. "Check!" Gladys hollered.

"Ah, she's a quick study, this one!" I heard Grandpa Ed say as I grabbed a piece of bacon from a plate in the kitchen and headed for the garage. Mom could only handle P.J. being inside for short periods of time—especially when his favorite foods were being served, and P.J. went nuts over bacon.

As soon as I opened the door to the garage, P.J.

rushed up, wagging his tail so hard his back legs skittered all over the place. He barked when he saw the strip of meat in my hand.

"Of course this is for you, boy," I said, crumbling the bacon and letting him eat out of my cupped palm. "Merry Christmas." I stroked his fur, let him lick my face, and told him I'd be back in a while.

The phone was ringing when I went back into the house.

I heard Mom pick up. She screamed.

I sprang up the stairs faster than the dad in "'Twas the Night Before Christmas."

Everyone was headed for the kitchen, where Mom stood shaking. "We've got a baby! We've got a *baby*!"

Dad put his arm around me as Mom continued to talk to the person on the other end of the line. Mary from the adoption agency, I supposed.

A baby. The thought made me feel full of wonder and something else, too. Not quite fear. But something headed in that direction. An unsure feeling—like when Grampa Clem and Gladys took me to the circus and I got up close to an elephant for the first time.

"Well, I'll be," Grandpa Ed said. "That's some kind of Christmas gift."

Gladys's hands covered her mouth. Her eyes had gotten watery. Dad went over and gave her a hug. She took off her glasses and wiped her eyes as Dad led her to the living room.

"All right. Thank you, Mary!" Mom hung up and wrapped me in her arms. "You've got a baby sister, Boo. What do you think about that?" She kissed the top of my head.

What I thought was that I didn't know the first thing about being a big brother. Would I be a good one? I was pretty sure I would, but now that the baby was actually coming, I realized I had some learning to do, and being a big brother probably wasn't the kind of thing I could research on the Internet.

Grandpa Ed followed Mom and me into the living room. Dad got up from the couch where he'd been sitting next to Gladys and hugged Mom. Grandpa Ed and I joined Gladys on the couch. She patted my leg. "Well, Edwin, we're getting ourselves another grandbaby." Gladys's face lit up with a smile. Even the corners of her wrinkles turned up.

"I only wish Caroline were here to see it," Grandpa Ed said. He pronounced her name "CARE-oh-line." "She would have been on cloud nine."

"My Clemons, too," Gladys said. She sniffed.

"Brendan," Mom said, her arms still wrapped around Dad's waist, "do you want to tell your grandparents your new sister's name?"

It was something I had come up with one night when Mom, Dad, and I were talking about the baby.

"Go ahead, Bren," Dad said.

I glanced at Grandpa Ed and then at Gladys. "My new little sister's name is Clementine . . . Caroline . . . Buckley." I grinned. The words felt exactly right coming out of my mouth, as if I'd been saying them all my life.

Gladys coughed. She thumped her chest a few times as if she'd accidentally swallowed the breath mint she'd been sucking; then she pulled out a wadded tissue and dabbed her eyes.

Grandpa Ed had cleared his throat a few times, as well, and Gladys held out a clean tissue.

"That's all right." He pulled out his handkerchief from his back pocket. "I'm always prepared."

"It's a perfect name," Gladys said, finally. She looked up. "Hear that, Clem? You got a granddaughter named after you. We're counting on you to be her guardian angel." She looked at Grandpa Ed. "Knowing that man, he pulled some strings for us to get this news on his birthday."

Mom told us more of the details then. The baby had actually been born on December 21, but the birth mom had just decided that morning to choose our family.

Seriously. What a Christmas present.

"I was thinking we could call her CeeCee for short," I said.

"CeeCee . . . ," Gladys said. "I like that. It's got attitude. Just like me."

While the adults continued to talk about the baby

and when we could go get her, I snuck away to my room.
I sat at my desk, flipped open my log, and wrote the date.

Log Entry—Tuesday, December 25—
Christmas Day/Grampa Clem's Birthday

I'm getting a baby sister. Her name is Clementine
Caroline. I sure hope I will do right by her. Khal's not
exactly a stellar role model in this area, but maybe
Morgan can help me. She's a girl, after all. And she
says she's really good with babies.

Dad and I had a good time fishing—I think we're
starting to understand each other a little better.

And I already know what I want to be when I'm
older—a scientist, of course—but who will I be? If I'm
someone like my dad, that'll be all right with me.

More Things I Learned About Biomass, Biogas, and the Future of Our Planet

By Brendan S. Buckley

- People in the United States produce 12,000 pounds of poop *per second,* or 518,400 tons a day.
- If you think that's a lot, livestock in the United States produces 25,000 pounds of poop per second! The average cow poops 100 pounds of feces a day (versus half a pound for humans)—the equivalent of 9 bowling balls. What if we converted all that biomass into *energy*?
- There are approximately 1.5 billion cows on earth. The energy in their manure could power 115 million cars, or 85 percent of the cars in the United States, and California's 1.7 million cows could power 120,000 homes.
- Biogas is a mixture of methane (same stuff as in natural gas) and carbon dioxide (CO_2)—both major causes of global warming. A big difference is that methane can also be used for fuel.

- Methane is released during the processing of natural gas and coal and by livestock when it produces gas and manure. Wetlands, oceans, and even termites produce methane naturally. However, methane traps about 21 times more heat in the atmosphere than CO_2 (a fact that can be attributed to the larger size of methane's molecules).

- Each cow on the planet produces anywhere from 100 to 500 liters of methane *per day*. (That's 50 to 250 two-liter soda bottles per cow!) In an effort to control greenhouse emissions, some countries are considering a "flatulence tax" on cows.

- Scientists are studying the gas of other animals to see if they burp methane-free gas. (I'd like to know how the scientists collect their samples.) They hope to come up with injections for cows that will promote the growth of stomach bacteria to eat up the methane from their gas.

- Biogas is considered a renewable resource because it's produced relatively quickly compared to natural gas, which forms over millions of years. Natural gas, used in most of our homes, is *not* considered a renewable form of energy.

- In nineteenth-century London, biogas was gathered from sewers to fuel streetlamps, which were called gaslights.

- In many parts of the world, biogas collected from both animal and human waste is heating and lighting homes, providing energy for cooking, even fueling buses. With all the excrement our exploding global population is producing, these countries could be on the cutting edge of alternative energy creation in the future!

- To learn more about biomass and biogas, visit this great website from the U.S. Energy Information Administration: eia.doe.gov/kids/energy.cfm?page=biomass_home-basics.

- If you'd like to do an experiment like mine and Morgan's, go to sciencebuddies.org and search for the experiment "From Trash to Gas: Biomass Energy." There are a lot of other cool experiments on this site that I plan to try.

- To build your own biogas generator, check out this website for construction plans: re-energy.ca/biogas-generator. Before you know it, you'll be cooking hash browns over a biogas flame. Good luck!

Important Things to Know About Green Anoles

By Brendan S. Buckley

Okay, so Einstein didn't make it, but I learned some things from my experience. Here are some tips for taking care of your green anole, plus some interesting facts:

- When anoles shed, they sometimes eat the skin.
- In the wild, anoles live less than 2.5 years. In captivity, they can live 3 to 6 years, with examples of up to 8 years. Unfortunately, most live less than 1 year because of owner ignorance. (Oops! That would be me.)
- Anoles reach adult size in 6 to 8 months.
- A male anole will extend his throat fan, or dewlap, when he wants other males to know they're stepping on his territory.
- In spite of what most people think, these lizards don't change color to match their surroundings. They change to *thermoregulate,* becoming darker when they're cold and lighter when they're too warm. When sleeping at night, they

adopt a light coloration, which makes them easy to collect with a flashlight. (Morgan told me this. She's actually done it.)

- Be sure to keep your anole in a glass tank with a screen top to provide adequate heating (plastic containers will melt under the lightbulbs your anole requires to stay warm). You want to have at least a 10-gallon tank (20 inches long by 12 inches high by 10 inches wide) to give your anole lots of space to run around.

- For a 10-gallon tank, you need a 40- to 60-watt bulb in a room kept at 70 to 74 degrees, assuming you've got a screen lid. The bulb should be in a reflector-type fixture.

- Your thermometer should read 85 to 90 degrees in your anole's basking spot. Daytime temps away from basking sites should be 75 to 80 degrees.

- Anoles can climb glass and will quickly escape from any uncovered enclosure. (I know all about this!)

- Spray your tank a couple of times a day with purified water (or you'll have hard-to-clean mineral deposits on the sides of the tank and plants). Humidity, measured with a hygrometer, should be kept at 50 percent or higher. Anoles drink water by lapping off leaves. They won't drink standing water unless trained to do so. To train them, set up a dripper over a dish of water.

- Your anole *is* what he or she eats, so you should only offer him the best! (Something I learned the hard way.) Commercially raised insects lose nutritional value during storage in a pet store. They should be gut-loaded with nutrients before you feed them to your anole. For example, put your crickets in a small plastic terrarium for 12 to 24 hours and offer them ground rodent chow, high-quality tropical fish flakes, or high-protein flaked baby cereal. For water and vitamin C, offer the crickets oranges. For beta-carotene, feed the crickets grated carrots. Then give the crickets to your anole the next day. Your lizards should stay healthier that way.

- Some anoles may become comfortable with being gently handled (like Einstein was after he got used to me). At first, though, all anoles will run from you when you go to pick them up, and they may bite (something Khal can tell you about). Biting, as much as it may hurt you, may be more dangerous for them if you jerk your hand away—this can break their jaws or cause teeth to be ripped out. So handle them as little as possible, and don't jerk your hand if you get bitten. Put them back in their enclosure so that they can feel something under their feet—that will get them to let go.

- They also can drop their tails if you grab them there (this is called autotomy), and their fragile toes can be broken or injured if they're removed too roughly from branches, bark, or your clothes.

- You know you've got a sick anole on your hands if he stops eating, or will not eat very much, or if he just sits there on your hand not trying to get away. Also look for loose skin and sunken eyes. But hopefully yours won't get sick. And hopefully I'll do better with Einstein Junior!

ACKNOWLEDGMENTS

Once again I have the opportunity to thank a cadre of people (one of my favorite parts of writing a book). They have helped make this story the best it could be. Thanks goes to the entire team at Delacorte Press, especially Michelle Poploff, Rebecca Short, Trish Parcell, and Ashley Mason, for being so responsive and invested. Thanks also to the school and library marketing team, led by the indomitable Adrienne Waintraub. Thank you to my agent, Regina Brooks, for continuing to believe in me, and to my ever-so-helpful and encouraging readers, Matt Frazier, Bethany Hegedus, Kekla Magoon, Fina Arnold, Micheline and Lala Lopez, and Kim and Ash Lawson.

I greatly appreciate my brother and sister-in-law, Isaac and Angie Tucker, who gave invaluable input on middle school dances (it's been a while since I attended one myself), and my nephew, Khalfani, for letting me use his name. Thanks, family.

To the many people who gave of their time and expertise, answering question after question so I could get the science and Tae Kwon Do elements of this story right (anywhere they're not right is all on me)—thank you for your passion for what you do and for your generosity in sharing your knowledge: the crew and scientists aboard the research vessel *Centennial*—Dr. David Duggins, Dr. Dennis Willows, Mr. Mark Anderson, Mr. Wolf

Krieger, and Dr. Uwe Brand; marine biologists Dr. David Secord and Dr. Cheryl Greengrove; for helping with pneumatic launchers, Dr. Scott Moor; Donna Hardy of sciencebuddies.org; educators John Weber, Ed Barrett, Kris Holmquist, and Andrew Song; the good folks at Midway Tropical Fish and Pets for letting me hold their green anole; and one giant *kam sa ham nida* to Nancy Henkel, fifth-degree black belt, whom I fondly refer to as my local Tae Kwon Do librarian.

Thanks to my dad, who would be the president of my fan club if I had one. And last but not at all least, because without them I truly could not get these books written, thank you to my husband and my mom for creating the space for me to pursue something I love to do.

SUNDEE T. FRAZIER wasn't planning to write a follow-up to her first novel, *Brendan Buckley's Universe and Everything In It*, but when she kept getting the question "Will there be a sequel?" she started asking whether there might be more to Brendan's story. Like Brendan, Sundee is interested in science, but she knows she is meant to be a writer. When she's not building pretend rocket ships or doing experiments with her two young daughters, she's writing from her home in the Seattle area. She is also the author of *The Other Half of My Heart*. You can read more about her and her work at sundeefrazier.com.

Praise for Sundee T. Frazier and
BRENDAN BUCKLEY'S UNIVERSE AND EVERYTHING IN IT

WINNER OF THE CORETTA SCOTT KING/JOHN STEPTOE
NEW TALENT AUTHOR AWARD

AN NCSS-CBC NOTABLE SOCIAL STUDIES
TRADE BOOK FOR YOUNG PEOPLE

A BANK STREET COLLEGE OF EDUCATION
BEST CHILDREN'S BOOK OF THE YEAR

WINNER OF A HORACE MANN UPSTANDERS
HONOR AWARD FOR CHILDREN'S LITERATURE

"Frazier writes affectingly about what being biracial means in twenty-first century America."   *—School Library Journal*

"Brendan is an appealing character with a sense of honor. . . . A good, accessible selection to inspire discussion of racism and prejudice."   *—Kirkus Reviews*

"Frazier delivers her messages without using an overly heavy hand. Brendan is a real kid with a passion for science and also a willingness to push his parents' rules."   *—Booklist*

READ BRENDAN BUCKLEY'S
FIRST ADVENTURE!

Ten-year-old Tae Kwon Do blue belt and budding rock hound Brendan Buckley keeps a CONFIDENTIAL notebook for his top-secret discoveries. And he's found something *totally* top-secret. The grandpa he's never met, whom his mom refuses to see or even talk about, is an expert mineral collector, and he lives nearby! Brendan sneaks off to visit his grandpa Ed DeBose, whose skin is pink, not brown like Brendan's, his dad's, and the late Grampa Clem's.

Brendan sets out to find the reason behind Ed's absence, but what he discovers can't be explained by science, and now he wishes he'd never found Ed at all. . . .